THE DOLLAR MAN

Also by Harry Mazer

GUY LENNY

SNOW BOUND

THE
DOLLAR MAN

HARRY MAZER

DELACORTE PRESS / NEW YORK

Third Printing—1975

Library of Congress Cataloging in Publication Data
Mazer, Harry.
The dollar man.

SUMMARY: *Raised by his mother, a fat
fourteen-year-old boy feels he must find his father
in order to establish his own identity.*
[1. FATHERS AND SONS—FICTION] I. TITLE.
PZ7.M47397DO [Fic] 73-17953

ISBN 0-440-03210-5

ONE

IT WAS DARK at six and the wind was blowing hard down East Broadway, where Marcus Rosenbloom stood near the bus stop waiting for his mother to come home from work. Despite the penetrating November chill, Marcus was hatless, his jacket thrown carelessly open as he leaned against the iron fence in front of the Beth Israel Home for the Aged. The young nurses, white shoes and long white legs gleaming, streamed out of the Home like a flock of shore birds in the gloom.

In the early evening shadow Marcus imagined himself an unseen watcher, nearly hidden in one of those thick white fogs that sometimes rolled over the low places in the city, blanketing streets and buildings and funneling the street lights. He imagined himself floating invisibly up into that fog, up between the buildings that lined East Broadway where the fog turned the lighted windows faint blue and lavender.

That was his "invisible" dream. It was one of his favorite dreams. In the dream he was transformed; no longer fat, stupid, or clumsy, he was athletic, muscular, lean as a bean—and invisible! In the dream he

1

was like his father, or what he thought his father was like. He'd never seen his father, not even a picture, except in dreams like these.

In the dream there might be a million people around him, but nobody could say no to him. Invisible Marcus was all powerful; he couldn't be kept out of any place in the world. He could go into any house, take any car, help himself to all the money he needed. As he'd once tried to explain to his best friend, Bernie McNutley, there were advantages to being invisible.

"If you're invisible, nobody can stop you. They can't see you, so they can't control you. They don't know where you are, they don't know what you're doing. You take something, they don't even know it's gone. Nobody can keep a count on all those things in the stores."

Bernie, who didn't believe in anything he couldn't hear, see, or step on, said Marcus was dead wrong. "They won't see you, but they'll see the things you take because things aren't invisible. You take a candy bar, or french fries, or a Kingburger, and they'll see it floating away." Bernie's brown eyes, from behind the circles of thick glasses, were calm and sure. "You take a car, they'll see it drive away."

"They won't see me. I'm Invisible Marcus who can go anywhere, do anything. I'll baffle the cops, the FBI, the State Troopers. They'll all be after me, but they'll never catch me."

Bernie didn't like the way Marcus was going to get away with things. That wasn't right. People had to work hard for what they got. His father went to work every day, and he worked overtime on Saturdays, and their car was seven years old and rusting away. "So why should you get a new car when nobody else can?"

"Because I'm invisible and I've got this invisible power that nobody else has."

"You'll maybe fool them once or twice, but that's all. Sooner or later, they're going to see you drive away in someone else's car, right? And they're going to figure out there's some kind of invisible nut behind the wheel."

"I'll be laughing my head off."

"Wait, wait—" Bernie sputtered, grabbing Marcus. "Wait'll I tell you. They see their car drive away, they're going to call the cops, right? And when the cops come—"

"I'm gone, split, vanished. I figured that out already." Marcus was triumphant. "They get the car back, but never the invisible me. I'll just go around the corner and take another car. There are a million cars to choose from. I take what I want, use it, and then put it back. Not too much. I won't be greedy. I won't hurt anyone either. I'll be a really honest crook. Just enough for myself and my friends, except good McNut, since he's so good, pure, and incorruptible."

Bernie planted himself squarely in front of Marcus. "You're going to get caught. That happens to every crook sooner or later. Your downfall is going to be food. Sometime, somebody's going to see this invisible thing grab a pie or a handful of candy bars, and he's going to get his arms around you, and hold you, and not let you go. The cops will come and they'll tie

3

you up, then they'll mark you with spray paint. Szzzzz! Szzzzz! Every inch of you outlined in indelible paint. Pink-colored. You'll stand out like a pink elephant, and that'll be the end of you."

"Okay, forget it," Marcus said, always sensitive to any reference to his size. "This conversation has become so boring it's stupid." After that he kept his invisible stories to himself.

Six-twenty on the revolving clock high over the gas station across the street, and his mother's bus still wasn't in sight. He peered down East Broadway, trying to distinguish the lights of the bus from other vehicles. He couldn't help worrying. What if something had happened to his mother? He knew he shouldn't let himself go this way. It was a habit from when he was little and staying in other people's apartments, waiting for her to come from work and take him home. In those days as soon as he started to feel hungry he knew she would be there soon, and then he couldn't wait till he heard her footsteps. He could tell his mother's steps anywhere. They didn't shuffle, slide, or scrape. Neat as a drumbeat, her footsteps beating a regular tattoo of heel leather on hard floors. It was always a beautiful clean sound.

The traffic coming from downtown was jammed solid into two long beeping lines of cars moving at a snail's pace. Across the street the wind whipped up the red and white flags outside the gas station. Marcus leaned his back against the iron railing, wrapped his fingers around the square rusty rods, squeezing with all his might. Squeeze and release, squeeze and release, that was the way to build up his strength and endurance. Then down to his toes for a toe stretch. Then hands over head, feet apart: jumping jacks, one-two-three-four, one-two-three-four . . .

The nurses were looking at him. He was tall for his age. In the dark they probably thought he was much older than his thirteen years—an athlete keeping in trim. He kept it up till he was out of breath. He felt better already, stronger and leaner. If he exercised like this every day he'd soon be in fantastic shape. Maybe he'd go down to the weight room at the Y and really start working out with the dumbbells.

Standing tall on the outside edges of his shoes, he imagined himself still taller, standing on stilts, seven feet high, tall as a Watusi. He was looking over everyone's head, stretching till he could look down East Broadway in either direction, his head up above the buildings, his chin resting on the rooftops; Marcus's big head over the city, watching over everyone. Spaghetti Man. It was like the Invisible Man fantasy, only now he was a rescuer—one of the good guys. Good Mr. Spaghetti, sliding up the sides of buildings, looking into windows for criminal acts, ever alert to the evil that lurked behind windows and walls. A quick glance and he moved away fast. If people saw him peering into windows it could scare them out of their minds. Give them heart attacks. Friendly Mr. Spaghetti didn't want to do that.

Mr. Spaghetti was part of a special Fire Department Rescue Squad, saving people that the fire ladders couldn't reach, people trapped in the new highrise buildings, people unable to go into the poisonous smoke-filled halls and elevators, waiting with their arms stuck out of windows and screaming for help.

"Mr. Spaghetti, Mr. Spaghetti!" He was in his special long, low, red, beetle-shaped car with the people scooper in front, and the special fire alarm band on the radio. A "Triple S All Zone Alarm" was a call for him. He flipped switches on his control panel, a warning light went on, a siren sounded to warn people and vehicles away. Mr. Spaghetti was on his way.

"Here comes Mr. Spaghetti, hurrah! Hurray!"

The fire chief was pacing up and down, chewing on his cigar. "Glad you're here, Spaghetti." He pointed to the seventy-seventh floor of the smoking skyscraper where no ladder could possibly reach. "There's a beautiful young girl up there, Spaghetti. We spotted her with our long-range opticals. The rescue helicopter can't maneuver in that close. You're our only hope."

Sliding back the clear plastic roof of his vehicle, Mr. Spaghetti listened carefully to the fire chief. From time to time he glanced up at the high-rise building. This was going to be a difficult assignment. He could stretch to the seventy-seventh floor, but he'd lose his elasticity. It would be like rolling clay out too fine. He wouldn't have the strength to hold the girl; he'd fall back on himself.

Tersely he questioned the fire chief. The elevators were all jammed, but he could get within twenty floors of the trapped girl. That was all he needed to know. He raced toward the building and up the stairs, fifty-seven floors up, taking them four at a

6

time. This was one time when his jumping-jack exercises came in handy.

When he emerged on the window ledge of the fifty-seventh floor, a distant roar rose up from below. He had time only for a quick wave to his admiring fans, then he turned to the rescue operation, anchoring his toes on the cement ledge, pointing his arms upward, parallel, his fingers flexed, stretching his elastic body until he touched and then encircled the girl's waist, being careful not to let his hands slip too high or too low as he gently brought her down to safety . . .

"Hello, Marcus, what are you trying to do?" It was his mother. "You look like you're off somewhere in space."

He became aware of himself standing against the iron fence with his arms stretched upward. "Waiting for you, Sally. You're late."

She was wearing a short dark coat over a plaid skirt. The wind whipped her hair across her face. She wore it long like a girl. He was taller than his mother now and growing more so every day. Her lips were warm against his cheek. She didn't smoke, but he could smell cigarette smoke in her hair.

"Marcus, your cheeks are cold and your hands are like ice. You shouldn't have come. It's so raw out." She straightened his collar, pulled down his sweater. "Your hair needs combing."

He ran his fingers through his hair. "Presto, combo. Beautiful, right, Sally?"

She took his arm. "You're a silly boy sometimes, but a joy."

Their first moments together were always so good, the way they always used to be and were so rarely now; friends, as much as mother and son. When he was little he used to play by a leaky fire hydrant, damming up the water with rocks and dirt, scooping out channels, rivers, and lakes. He'd make twigs into trees, and on the banks of his river he'd make houses out of pebbles and bridges out of Fudgcicle sticks. When he came home filthy his mother would put him in the tub and clean him up herself. She thought it was amusing, a boy needed dirt. She said, "Did you build a beautiful big city? Someday you'll build a real city."

She bought him blocks and a construction set, and encouraged him to build things. Sometimes she'd sit and watch him building, asking him what this or that was. He liked building for his mother, liked doing things for her. It was always that way before they started being strange with each other. Maybe it really was all his fault. Lately he couldn't predict his feelings—perfect friends one minute, and then she'd say something and he'd flare up for no reason.

But now, arm in arm, like the best of friends, they went clomping down the wooden sidewalks along the fenced-off sections of East Broadway where the old mansions had been torn down to make room for new high-rise apartment projects. His mother had been involved in a failed effort to save Duckworth House, a white Greek Revival mansion with wide porches and tall fluted columns. All that remained now was a mound of earth where grass and weeds grew wild.

"People, where do they all come from, Marcus?"

his mother said, telling him about her working day at the State Employment Office, about the steady, endless, unsettling streams of people who came into her office. "All day long. By two this afternoon I was ready to scream, I was sick of seeing people. I know it isn't a very nice thing to say. We're supposed to be helping people, but there are so many of them and they all have families, they all need jobs. I feel they all want something from me that I can't give them."

She often spoke this way at the end of a tiring day. "When you're tired," she said, "everything looks awful."

He said, "Get another job if this one is bugging you, Sally. Rossi pays me five dollars for delivering groceries Friday night. I'll ask him for more time. You could do a lot of things."

"Oh, I know, but despite everything I feel, I know we do some little bit of good. You can't turn your heart off with people, then you will become a machine, and that would be the end of everything."

A man stood aside to let them pass, looked at his mother, then looked at him. *Bug off,* Marcus wanted to tell him, *that's my mother, and I'm her son, and we're going home to my father who's big and strong and lifts pianos for exercise. If he catches you looking at my mother, he'll break you in two . . .*

"Bill will be here in a few days," his mother said. "What should we have for supper when he comes?" They stopped for the light on Columbus Avenue, then crossed to the Shopping Plaza. Bill Brenner, his mother's friend—his, too—a free-lance musician, a first-chair trumpet player, a teacher, an arranger and

9

composer of music, a traveling man who came and went in their lives. Sometimes on school mornings, after not seeing Bill for months, Marcus would find him asleep on the couch, bony feet sticking out from under a blanket, his suitcases and trumpet case and bundles thrown down in the hall.

"Bill," Marcus said, "will eat anything you put in front of him on a plate. He's that grateful for a real meal."

"Oh, he's got more taste than that. I thought you two men would have a preference. Steak? A roast? I hate to always have to decide."

The Shopping Plaza was brightly lit, the three-acre lot crowded with cars and people streaming in and out of the stores. Between the parking lot and the stores there was a long wedge of green benches and a round concrete fountain where teen-agers liked to congregate. Marcus saw some of the older kids from school there: Phillips, Bisner, a couple of girls, and on the back of a bench sitting higher than the others, like a king, was Dorrity.

"Hey, Rosey, who's your girl friend?" one of the boys called.

Marcus looked up in surprise. In school he didn't think they knew he even existed, especially Dorrity, whom Marcus had admired from a distance. Dorrity, who seemed so relaxed, easy, and sure of himself, every quality that Marcus thought he lacked.

His mother paused, and smiled. "Your friends? Stop and talk if you like. I'll take care of the shopping."

Suddenly he was furious. Why was she telling him

what to do? If he wanted to stop, he'd stop. He didn't need her telling him. "I'm going with you!" But immediately he felt disgusted with himself, cowardly, aware of the way he was hanging onto his mother's arm as if he were afraid to let go of her. Dorrity, who he was sure was watching everything, must think he was a baby.

He shook loose, walking away from her. "Go ahead, Sally. You don't need me to help you shop. Get anything you want. I'll wait for you out here."

His mother left, and he stood scuffing at the curbstone, unable to look directly toward Dorrity and the others, afraid to approach them—what could he possibly say to Dorrity?

Later that night Marcus and Sally made a cake together. That is, his mother made the cake while he whipped up a gooey, thick, coffee-flavored chocolate icing to spread on it, once it was cooled. Then they sat together to sample it, his mother sipping tea while he had a quart of milk next to his plate. His mother cut a thick slice of cake and divided it unevenly, giving the larger piece to Marcus. He took big bites of the crumbly sweet cake, with long swallows of cold milk.

"This is as good a cake as I've ever eaten," he said expansively.

"Your icing is smooth as butter," his mother said.

"Thank you, Sally."

"You're welcome, Marcus."

Anything sweet, that was his weakness, and his mother didn't take his efforts to diet seriously. But now wasn't the time to think about his weight. He took another slice of cake, washing it down with milk, enjoying a reckless, abandoned feeling.

"What do your friends say, Marcus—the funny ones on the bench. Do they ever ask about me? What do you tell them?"

He gathered the crumbs together on his plate and swallowed them. "I tell them to mind their own business."

His mother looked at him dubiously. "You don't really say that, do you? Are you that defensive?"

"I was just kidding," Marcus said.

"I've always wanted you to be straightforward about us," his mother said. "If anyone asks me, I tell them, yes, my son and I live alone. No, I'm not married, and no, I never was married. It's the best way— straightforward and honest."

"Sure," Marcus said. "I do that. If someone asks me a question about my family, I answer them. I say I live with my mother. If they ask about my father, I say he doesn't live with us."

"Is that all you say?"

"What else is there to say?" He met her eyes carefully and evenly, but then he looked down, running his finger round and round the red rim of his plate. His mother had never told him anything about his father—not even his name. When kids started talking about their mothers and fathers, Marcus was always on guard for the questions that might follow about his own mother and himself and how they lived, and where was his father? When other kids talked about their fathers and asked where was *his* father, what could he say? When his mother said, "Your father was nothing in your life, so why should I build him up in your eyes?" Marcus understood. But you couldn't tell other kids stuff like that. And you couldn't just stand around like a dope when kids started talking about their fathers doing this and that. Marcus had to say something, too.

It wasn't hard. He'd always told himself stories about his father, in bed at night, or in the morning, just daydreaming. In his head it was like the pictures in a comic book; his father was always the hero, with the little captions above his head: "Don't worry, Mr. President. I've got this revolution down here in the Islands under control, sir."

A lot of the kids were putting it on for sure, bragging how strong their fathers were, or how they'd won the war singlehanded. So he did, too. He'd say, "I'm not allowed to talk about my father's job. He's away most of the time—Secret Government work . . ." And he'd build his stories, telling how his father had once brought home a wild horse he'd broken and they kept it in a stable in another neighborhood. Or how his father had brought home a boa constrictor from an Amazon expedition, and they kept it in the bathtub till one day it had disappeared down the drain.

It was stupid telling those stories about his father. He knew the kids looked at him like he was crazy, disbelief on their faces, openly making fun of him. "Yeah! Yeah! Tell us more!" He was called a liar, a big mouth, and the fattest BS artist in school.

Every time he told one of his stories he promised himself never again, and then someone would say, *My father did this*, or *My father did that*, and he'd feel they were all looking at him, snickering, laughing because he didn't have a father. And before he could stop himself, he'd be saying, "My father isn't home now. The Pentagon called him—a Four Star General. He wanted my father to fly right down to Washington . . ."

Even when he saw kids punch each other, or heard them snort derisively, he couldn't turn off his mouth.

"When I was a girl," Sally said, "we kids talked about our parents all the time."

"Kids still do," Marcus said. He could brag about Sally any day of the week. That's what he ought to do. Sally was special, different from other mothers. She did everything the mothers who stayed home did, and she worked, too. He was proud of the way he and Sally lived together: she always treated him like a real person. Nobody else lived the way he and Sally did. He didn't miss his father either. The stories he made up, the daydreams and fantasies were just make-believe, something that happened inside him when he wasn't doing anything or thinking about anything in particular.

"I was so curious about everybody else's life when I was a girl," Sally said, smiling at him. "Don't you feel that way, Marcus? Don't you want to know how other people live? I bet plenty of your friends ask about that tall man they see you walking around with."

"Yes, sometimes," he said, fiddling with the empty milk carton. He never had any trouble talking about Bill. Bill was his mother's friend, and his friend, too. He liked Bill, and Bill liked him. He never made up stories about Bill. Why should he? Only about his father.

TWO

AFTER SCHOOL Marcus and Bernie stopped at the Prescott Street playground and headed over to where the monkey bars stood in a sand pit. Marcus leaned against the stone wall while Bernie swung the length of the horizontal ladder, hand over hand, legs working, turning at the end without resting and coming back the other way. Bernie was short and compact and he could do things with his body that Marcus envied. Bernie chinned himself on the bar, then swung over the top and somersaulted down, landing with his arms akimbo like a circus performer.

"You do it, Marc," he said.

Marcus looked around. He didn't want anyone watching. He wasn't good at this stuff. He got on the first rung, grasping the bar over his head. Then he looked again to see that nobody was around. Little kids didn't matter.

"Let go," Bernie said. "Grab the next bar."

Marcus told his hands to let go, but nothing happened. He just hung there, kicking his feet, while his arms felt as if they were being pulled out of their sockets. His grip loosened. His hands were slipping off the cold steel bar.

"Hold on," Bernie urged.

He couldn't hold on. He let go and dropped to the sand pit. "My hands were slippery," he said, rubbing sand on his palms.

"Try it again," Bernie directed. "Do it till you build up your strength." And to show Marcus how easy it was, he sprang up to the ladder and swung across from bar to bar like a monkey.

Marcus got mad at himself for being so sloppy, fat-ass lazy. He grabbed the bar and hung on, thrashing his feet, yelling at himself to let go and grab the next bar. Nothing happened. He couldn't budge. He hung there like a limp bag of sand.

"You can do it," Bernie said enthusiastically, getting under Marcus and grasping him around the knees, taking most of the weight off Marcus's arms. "Now do it, Marc, let go with one hand and grab the other bar."

A spray of gravel and dirt rained down on them. It was thrown by skinny Willis Pierce, standing at the fence and hanging onto the wire like a spider. "Hey, Bernie, you teaching Fat Man how to be an ape?"

Marcus let go of the bar, bringing both him and Bernie crashing to the ground. Willis Pierce had been in almost every class with Marcus from Prescott Street to Columbus Junior High, a thorn in Marcus's side, the bane of his life, the person he hated most in the world.

"If you don't have anything good to say," Bernie said, getting up and brushing himself off, "don't say anything."

"Who's talking to you, retard?" Willis said. "I was

talking to your elephant friend. Jump on those bars again, Rosen Balloon, I want to see you bend them."

Marcus turned his back on Willis. He'd promised himself not to be everyone's Laughing Fat Boy anymore. In Prescott Elementary, whenever the teacher left the room, the other students would practically fall off their seats laughing as Willis waddled around imitating Marcus, holding his arms away from his body and blowing out his cheeks. "Clump, clump, clump, this is the way you look, Rosen Balloon," Willis would huff, slapping his feet down heavily on the floor. "Everyone head for the hills! Here comes Marcus the Elephant!"

And Marcus, sitting in back, arranging and rearranging his books, pyramiding them with his heavy notebook on the bottom and his ballpoint pen on top, feeling the sly, bright eyes of his classmates on him, would look up, open his mouth, and widen his eyes, the jolly fat schoolboy, grinning and laughing. And all the time he was laughing he thought what a stupid idiot he was, what a dumb, uncontrollable moron, a coward who didn't even have the nerve not to laugh at himself.

"I have to watch myself every minute, Mrs. Pennock," Willis told the teacher. "Every time Marcus sees me he tries to step on me with his huge feet."

"That's not very nice," the teacher said. "I think it's extremely unfair for a person your size, Marcus, to pick on a person Willis's size."

"That's right," Willis said, sliding around on his seat and facing Marcus, "that's very unfair, Marcus."

Willis was mocking Mrs. Pennock and she was

taken in. It was incredible how Willis could do anything to people and get away with it. Because he was
so small and skinny, people felt sorry for him, while
everything Marcus did was magnified ten times. He
was always noticed because he was enormous, and
if he tried to hide he only looked ridiculous.

He'd hoped that once he entered Columbus Junior
High his life would change. The Boulevard bus that
he took every day was a portent of a new life. A new
school, new teachers, new classmates. He dreamed of
a whole new world where he would be perceived
differently—the New Marcus. He hardly knew who
that New Marcus was, only that he was someone
better and finer.

On orientation day that fall he'd sat in the dimness
of the auditorium dreaming of his new self peeling
off his obese ugliness, like a skin diver peeling off a
rubber suit. Inside he wasn't what kids thought he
was, at all. He was like the prince taking off his rusty
helmet before the royal court, stepping out of his old
clanky, stiff suit of armor. Everybody would be
speechless, struck dumb. Well, that's how dumb he'd
been. Because when the lights went on, his daydreams were shattered. Willis and his cohorts were
there waiting for Marcus.

"Look what they let in . . . look what got loose,"
they said, cheerfully calling to each other in mock
wonder. "This isn't a school. It's a zoo!"

Marcus had ambled easily up the center aisle right
into the middle of his tormentors, nodding and smiling, and swatting playfully at them as he passed. He
even did the Jolly Fat Boy Shuffle for them, dancing

through the group, his arms swinging, and then going and going, and not looking back. Finally he made himself a promise that he was never going to break. No more Jolly Fat Boy. That much he could do for himself . . .

Beneath the monkey bars he turned to Bernie, deliberately not looking at Willis. "Come on, let's go," he said. They left the playground.

Bernie's home was on the ground level of a six-story apartment building crowded between two other apartment buildings. Bernie unlocked the entrance door just inside a long dark corridor, and he and Marcus stepped into a still darker apartment hallway. Vivian, Bernie's older sister, switched on the light. She was wearing a striped red and white tank shirt and blue jeans, with her thick dark hair wound into a heavy rope hanging over one shoulder. She was taller than her brother, but not as tall as Marcus. She had thick straight brows and wide, perfectly blue eyes, exactly the color of Bernie's eyes when he had his glasses off. The resemblance between Bernie and Vivian interested Marcus. They looked so much alike and at the same time were so different.

"Bernie, and Bernie's big-little friend," Vivian said breezily, as she preceded them down the dark hallway. "Where have you two kids been? Mom told me to wait and make sure you didn't gorge yourself on sweets, kiddies."

Bernie went straight to the cookie jar that was shaped like a fat white rabbit and grabbed it by its rabbit ears cover. "We got any sugar wafers left, or did you gobble them all?" He looked inside. "Empty!

Nothing left! Not a crumb. You ate the last one," he accused his sister.

"And did you a favor, sugar baby. Now there's nothing to tempt you."

"I'm tempted to pop you on the nose," Bernie said.

Bernie and Vivian were always like this, neither giving an inch, teasing each other constantly. Marcus was fascinated. He didn't think they really meant it, but then he wasn't quite sure. Having been raised as an only child he couldn't really tell how much was real, and how much just teasing.

Bernie, on the way to the bathroom, said, "Take anything you want, Marc. Take bread and jam. Take milk. And don't listen to her. She just lives here. She's not the boss."

Alone with Vivian, Marcus felt ill at ease. He put down the bread he'd been sweetening. He didn't want her to think he ate like a pig. He rubbed his hands together and adjusted his belt.

Vivian looked at him pleasantly and told him to fix himself a sandwich. "I just snarl at my brother, nobody else. He's got to be kept in his place. I'm really very nice."

"I'm on a diet," Marcus said. "I'm getting in shape. Maybe I'll go out for the wrestling team."

"Diet!" she said. "What for? You're big, you've got big bones. You're fine the way you are."

"Yeah, yeah," he murmured, flustered and flattered, aware of the way his body was flashing hot and cold down his spine. His burning ears must be glowing like two Christmas lights. "I've got to get in shape. I'm too heavy." Nervously he reached up and gripped the top of the doorframe. He thought he might practice hanging, but decided not to.

"Nobody in this family can stretch that high," Vivian said admiringly. "You want a rag to clean the woodwork?"

Marcus looked at his smudged fingers and wiped them on the side of his pants. "It sure needs it."

"Now you've done it, Marcus! When my mother comes home I'll tell her the building inspector was here, and what you said."

"God, don't do that!" He really liked Vivian's sense of humor, it was like his own, exaggerating things till they were comical. At the same time he wasn't used to joking with girls, except for Wendy Barrett and she didn't count. "Your mother will throw me out and never let me darken your door again."

"A lot you'd care," Vivian said. "You'd go to somebody else's house to eat. There's no loyalty anymore. Anybody who has the biggest cookie jar and the most goodies—"

"I'm loyal," Marcus said. "I'm one hundred percent loyal to the McNutleys, Bernie Nut and all the rest of the Nuts."

"It's a good thing you said that, Marcus." She came up to him standing in the doorway and tapped him on the shoulder. "Or you would have made me lose my faith in the human race."

He turned his head, worried about his breath and the way he smelled. She was standing so close to him he was aware of the shine of her nose and the pores in her skin. "You're big," she said. "How tall are you, anyway?"

Marcus put his hands in his pockets. "Five foot eleven and a half."

She whistled. "Nearly six feet! You'll be a giant some day. You'll be so big you won't speak to the rest of us. You'll be so big we'll all be invisible." She shook her head. "And you still haven't reached your full growth. You're already bigger than all the boys in my class. How tall's your father?"

"I don't know. I'm tall because my mother is tall."

"Oh, she's not that tall," Vivian said. "I've seen your mother. I bet it's your father. He must be over six feet—"

Marcus started for the hall. "Bernie!" he yelled. "I'll wait for you outside." He was mad. Vivian had burned him by wisecracking about his father. She must know he didn't know beans about his father. Bernie must have told her.

Vivian grabbed his jacket. "Hey, Marcus, don't go away. I hurt your feelings. I'm sorry. Come on, don't be mad."

He shook his head. "My feelings don't get hurt that easy. When my feelings get hurt you'll know it. You can say anything to me, and it wouldn't hurt my feelings."

She held his sleeve, pulling him back toward the kitchen. "Don't be mad, or I'll feel terrible. I embarrassed you, didn't I, talking about how big you are and how big your father is. I know your parents were never married. I didn't mean to hurt your feelings. I've got a big mouth and a mean streak a mile wide. But I really like talking to you. We won't talk about your father if it bothers you."

"It doesn't bother me," he said loftily, letting himself be drawn back into the kitchen.

"Not knowing your father, you probably never even think about him, do you?"

That wasn't exactly true. He was tempted to tell her he thought about his father a lot more than anyone knew. He had a lot more questions than he'd ever asked. His mother wouldn't talk about his father, and he still hadn't gotten up the nerve to question his grandmother or Bill. So he mostly daydreamed about his father, what he must look like, and whether he was like him in any way. There were the times when he thought he'd sighted his father, and the times he felt his father was very close to him. He'd never told these things to anyone. Bernie, being so practical-minded, would only have given him reasons why he was crazy. But Vivian was different. She'd be interested in his stories. Like that day at the demonstration in Washington when he'd half believed he'd found his father.

The demonstration had something to do with teachers and getting more money for schools. His mother's friend Grace Barrett was a teacher, and she and her daughter Wendy had gone to Washington with Marcus and Sally. He must have been really little, because one moment he was holding his mother's hand and the next moment he was lost somewhere in front of the Washington Monument with a million people pressed around him, and his mother gone—and all he could see were legs and coats and boots. He wasn't scared. He'd never been scared in crowds. There was room to move around, wriggle between people, and go tunneling through the crowd, looking up at people and trying to see his mother. When he heard his name called over the loudspeakers, he was delighted.

"Marcus Rosenbloom, come to the speaker's platform, your mother is waiting for you. Marcus Rosenbloom . . . Marcus Rosenbloom . . ."

He thought his name was being heard over the whole city of Washington. Maybe the President heard it, and all those senators and other people his mother and "Aunt" Grace and their friends were trying to get to listen to them.

"Marcus Rosenbloom . . . Marcus Rosenbloom . . ." His name bounced off the Washington Monument and rolled out over all those official buildings in the big city.

"Here I am," he said, squeezing through between coats and legs. "Here I am. Here's Marcus Rosenbloom," he said, raising his hand. "Here, here, here!"

"Here he is," somebody said. "Are you Marcus?" A man put Marcus on his shoulders so he was higher than everyone else. The man had thick curly black hair and enormous red ears that Marcus hung onto. When Sally saw the two of them, she waved and smiled radiantly at the man as if he were someone really wonderful. That was when Marcus had the feeling that the man who had picked him up must be his father, and now that they were with Sally the three of them would go someplace together to eat and talk.

He was tempted to tell Vivian that story. But she had already started talking about something else. "You're not like my brother," she said. "He can't sit

24

down and talk to a girl the way you can. He can't listen to anything a girl says."

"Girls are people," Marcus said.

She tapped him on the arm. "Tell it to Bernie. He thinks girls are another species."

"A low animal species," Bernie agreed, appearing in the doorway. "Why don't you leave my friend alone?"

"What do you mean, *your* friend?" Vivian said. "Marcus is my friend." She made a Swiss cheese and mustard sandwich on wheat bread and insisted that Marcus sit down next to her at the kitchen table and share it. Marcus tried to act matter-of-fact about the whole thing. He tried to catch Bernie's eye to indicate he was just going along with Vivian. But Bernie was eating a peanut butter and jelly sandwich and concentrating on a comic.

"What do you think, Marcus?" Vivian said, putting her hand to her hair. "Should I cut my hair? Do you like the way I look?"

"You'd scare a dead horse at midnight," Bernie said, without looking up from his comic.

"Who asked you? I was talking to my good friend Marcus."

"He's too polite to tell you the truth." Bernie got to his feet and tucked the comic in his hip pocket. "Let's go, Marc. She'll clean up. It's girl's work."

"Hey!" Vivian flared. "That's too much! You clean up your own mess."

"Let's work together," Marcus suggested. He was used to cleaning up.

"Whose side are you on?" Bernie demanded. "Come

25

on, you've got the wrong attitude. Girls do kitchen work. They're used to doing it while boys go out to play. Come on." He started to go. But Vivian, moving with surprising speed, got between him and the door and blocked the hallway, her arms touching both walls.

"You're not getting through till you put things away, Bernie McNutley!"

Bernie put his head down like a wild buffalo getting ready to charge, and Vivian stood there like nothing would ever move her.

"Come on, Bernie, don't be an idiot," Marcus said. He was afraid they'd really fight. "This is really getting stupid. What's the big deal about putting a few things away? I don't mind doing it."

"Do it then," Bernie said. "I'm not doing girl's work!"

"Okay," Marcus said, turning to Vivian. "What do you want me to do?" He was relieved. "Where do things go?"

But Vivian wasn't letting her brother off that easily. She was enjoying herself too much. She looked at her brother through narrowed eyes. "Since you're so superior, we'll settle this with a contest. I'm challenging you to a fight. The winner doesn't have to clean up."

"I'm not fighting with you. You'd just go crying to Mom if you lost," Bernie said. "You'd say I was picking on you."

"And I'm not fighting you," Vivian said. "You're not my equal. I'm going to hand-wrestle Marcus. If he wins, I'll do the whole clean-up, but if I win, *you* do it, Bernie McNutley."

Bernie went back into the kitchen. "Start cleaning," he told his sister, "because you're going to lose. Nobody moves Man Mountain Rosenbloom."

Marcus didn't say it, but he thought the same thing. He was bigger and heavier than Vivian; besides, he was a boy and good in Indian wrestling. Of course, they were all pretty good athletes in the McNutley family, but he didn't think she could break his grip. She'd made a losing bet and he was willing to let the challenge drop. He didn't really want to beat her.

"Look," he said, putting up his hands, "this isn't exactly fair. I'm bigger and heavier."

"Do you want to fight or talk?" Vivian demanded. "If he doesn't fight," she said to her brother, "you do the whole clean-up. Right now!"

"Fight," Bernie said to Marcus, "and knock her flat on her buttons."

There was nothing he could do. They faced off in the narrow hallway, foot to foot, grasping each other's hands. Marcus was surprised how strong Vivian's grip was; when he tried to snap her wrists and pull her over, she gave way slowly. She looked him straight in the eye, her lips pressed together, with the same look Bernie got when he and Marcus were wrestling, her eyebrows almost touching with determination.

Marcus still thought it was a joke. He put his weight against hers, feeling her give way reluctantly. He had only to keep up the pressure, wait for her to go off balance and move her feet. That would be the end. Her face was almost touching his, there the heat of her cheek, the clean smell of her skin, and her hand squeezing his hand. He was surprised

27

how far back she went without losing her balance. She was full of surprises, as flexible as a rubber band.

"Marcus," Bernie yelled, "Wake up! If you let her beat you—!"

But there was nothing Marcus could do about it. Somehow he was losing his balance, while she was still balancing easily. To keep from falling off his feet, he had to step forward, and so he lost.

"I won," Vivian cried, clapping her hands together triumphantly. "I won." She patted Marcus on the shoulder. "You did your best, but I'm the winner. The best woman won."

Bernie was disgusted. "If I had known you'd fall over and play dead, I'd never have let you do it."

Marcus, however, didn't feel like a loser. He couldn't stop looking at Vivian. She was really amazing. He felt fantastic, as if his eyes were open, really open, for the first time.

"It was fair all right," Vivian said triumphantly, still goading her brother. "While you work," she told him, "my friend and I are going to sit and have an intelligent conversation. I like you, Marcus," she went on, linking arms with him. "You're tall, you're husky. You've got a nice straight nose and curly hair. You've got an interesting face!"

He felt she must still be teasing, but there was nothing he could do about it. He knew he would always love her.

THREE

MARCUS WOKE in the morning with damp sheets wound tightly around his body. At first he thought he'd wet the bed. God! But he never did that anymore. Then he remembered about wet dreams. Some time ago his mother had told him about the changes that boys and girls both went through in puberty, how body hair grew, and girls got breasts, and boys' voices deepened and they had nighttime emissions. The changes were slower in some and faster in others, she said, but they were natural and inevitable. She was willing to talk to him about any aspect of his changing development. "Maybe you and Bill and I could sit down together sometime and talk."

But Marcus didn't feel the need for talk. He knew about sex and the changes. Everybody knew it.

Hurriedly, afraid his mother would see, he stripped the bed and buried the sheets in the bottom of the hamper. Then he turned on the shower and stood in the tub, letting warm water pour over his head. He used to take tub baths. His friend Bernie still did, carelessly leaving the door unlocked. Not Marcus. Not since he became aware of himself and the way his thing grew unpredictably, popping up like a seal in the water. *Push it down and dive . . . Commander Cousteau taking the submarine down six fathoms . . . watch out for sharks below, men, we're diving . . .*

His mother had almost caught him once. He'd barely had time to sit up and snatch a washcloth, his cheeks burning. After that he started locking the door and taking showers.

Holding onto the top of the shower fixture, he let the spray hit him full in the face, hardening his skin. Then he lay down in the long old-fashioned tub, hands behind his head, and let the water beat on his chest while he raised himself to a sitting position. Up and down, up and down, up and down till his stomach muscles ached. If he did that twice a day it would make a difference. The important thing was to have a plan and exercise every day. And stop eating so much. He flopped over and with the water splashing off his back did several push-ups, concentrating on his arms and gut.

"Marcus, are you all right in there?"

He jumped, sure he'd been caught.

His mother rattled the doorknob. "Marcus, do you hear me?"

"Yes! I'm in here."

"I'm going to work now. Don't be late for school. I'll see you tonight."

"Okay, Sally." He shut off the water. As he combed his hair he heard his mother leave. He was alone in the apartment, as he was often alone when his mother was working. Alone, he always felt a little sorry for himself, but also free, unrestrained, and slightly abandoned.

In the kitchen he caught a glimpse of the remains of last night's chocolate cake. There was no price for a single slice. It washed down deliciously with cold milk as he read the sports page. More milk, another slice of cake, all the good resolutions pushed away for later. He read the funnies, then the letters on the editorial page, and studied the political cartoon, all the time absently slicing and eating the cake. Slice after slice, leaning on one knee on the chair till there was nothing left.

He stared down at the empty cake plate. He never knew when to stop. He was stuffed. Uuuch! He bunched his shirt up in front to hide the bulge. It was still there, pressing against the cloth, an undisguisable tire of rubbery meat. He'd like to slice it off like the butcher Rossi slicing fat. He couldn't stand himself. Disgusted, he hit himself in the gut, blaming himself for being piggish, and then blaming his mother for making the cake and leaving it around to tempt him.

He cleared the table. Everything was a mess. The empty milk carton into the garbage, dirty dishes into the sink, newspaper folded on the chair, a quick swipe at the table with a rag. His disgust with himself colored everything. He flung the rag into the open cupboard, splat! around the box of breakfast cereal. Eating, eating, eating, he couldn't control his beastly habits. He ate like a machine, automatically opening his mouth when food was in front of him. Pro-

grammed like a computer. His mind turned off, his
mouth turned on.

How could Vivian like him when he looked like a
fat rubber tire? Oh, Viv! Was he ever going to
change? Eat less, and exercise more, lose weight and
develop some muscles, show some real self-control
and will power. Not be the same slob he'd always
been!

Getting ready for school, he made more stern resolutions. This time—today, *now*—he was going on a
diet and sticking to it. He'd cut out lunch, no snack
after school, and only a light supper. Making plans
was good. A plan was something you did step by
step; nothing important was changed just by wish-
ing!

Skipping lunch would be easy and cutting out
snacks after school—he could do it if he was determined and had the will power. He had it, he knew
that he did. He felt strong and good. As he left for
school, he began to feel positively euphoric. Walking
toward the bus stop he caught glimpses of himself
reflected in store windows and in the glass of cars.
Marcus imagined a tall, active, vital figure, long legs
and a large head made bigger by the thick curls of
black hair. Weren't people turning to look at him as
he passed? Women, and girls, and men, too.

He saw the same look reflected in the bus driver's
gold pilot glasses; the man really admired the way
Marcus snapped out his bus pass and stepped smartly
to the rear. No trouble with that boy! Women sitting
on the aisle looked as he passed—older women in
cloth coats with their large shopping bags and sad,

powdery faces. He'd often felt they'd like to have a son like him.

And two girls sitting close together, their knees touching, were whispering about him behind their fingers. They were looking at him, too. He sucked in his stomach, standing tall, his head almost brushing the top of the bus.

On the long back seat he recognized two of Dorrity's friends, Phillips and Bisner. He sat down next to them. "Hi," he said, "where's Dorrity?"

Bisner sat with his legs apart, his jeans worn white at the knees. "Get your fat ass over and don't hog the whole seat," he said. Phillips smiled maliciously.

Marcus's face burned as he moved over. He looked out the window as if he didn't care and tried to get back those good feelings about himself. He should have told Bisner to bug off, to go chase his tail, told him he was the biggest hog of them all . . .

Long before lunchtime, Marcus was starved. Normally he would have gone through his lunch from home by midmorning and been ready for a second lunch in the cafeteria. The acid smell of soggy sauerkraut and the thought of long, water-swollen franks were driving his gastric juices into a frenzy. The lunch line stretched out into the corridor and around the corner. Bernie had gone ahead to save a couple of seats in the cafeteria, while Marcus stood in line to buy milk and ice cream for his friend. He was going to stick to tomato soup and crackers.

Ahead of him in line were Bisner, Phillips, and Dorrity, plus a couple of girls. He recognized Flo

Weaver from his English class. But it was Dorrity he watched. Dorrity was their leader. He felt the others did whatever Dorrity said, no questions asked. He'd seen them together in the lunchroom, always at the same table by the window. Dorrity was always at the center. When Marcus entered school he'd see them at the head of the main stairs, Dorrity taller than the rest, a tight little knot that people had to walk around to get by—even the teachers.

Marcus returned to the table with his bowl of tomato soup and cellophaned package of crackers. Bernie frowned as he watched Marcus crumble and empty the crackers into his soup. "That all you're eating, Marc?"

"I'm on a diet," Marcus said. "If I can hold out long enough, I'm going to get into good shape."

Bernie took a huge bite out of his egg salad sandwich, dripping mayonnaise down his chin. "Stay with it," he said through a mouthful of food, "when you're fat, the only way to make that fat disappear is to eat less."

Marcus raised his bowl, licking up the last drops of the thin soup. "I feel empty," he said. "Really empty and weak."

"That's good. Hunger pangs means your body is calling for food. But if you don't eat, your body will start digging into that stored-up mass of fat."

Marcus wished Bernie wouldn't keep emphasizing that word—fat. He watched as Bernie unwrapped a huge, fluffy pink cake that seemed to Marcus in his weakened condition to be half the size of the table. He stared balefully at Bernie. Him and his unasked-for advice. Marcus was starving, but did Bernie care? No, he went right on stuffing himself with enough food to feed both of them. When Bernie got up for a second ice cream sandwich, Marcus had to leave the lunchroom. Otherwise he would have snatched the ice cream out of his friend's mouth and consumed it in a couple of famished bites.

That afternoon was an incredible ordeal. He couldn't concentrate on anything in school. Food! He wanted food! When he left school his head was spinning. He was hungry. He was starving. He was so weak he wondered if he'd make it home. He was used to eating every day, four times a day, five times a day, any time he wanted to.

He knew he was exaggerating, driving himself crazy. Nobody had to eat every minute. Think of all the people in the world who barely had enough to eat once a day. The desperately poor of the world, the individuals trapped in terrible situations of deprivation, going without food for weeks and weeks. Why couldn't he control himself for a few hours?

But the more he tried not to think about food the more impossible it became. On the bus going home after school, his eyes swung hungrily from shop window to shop window; every store on Columbus Avenue was crammed with food. Marcus tore his eyes away from the stores only to have them transfixed by tempting placards above his head advertising savory hotdogs, hero sandwiches, and foaming chocolate malteds. He closed his eyes to resist temptation, only to smell chewing gum and then garlic. He heard a baby sucking a bottle, a kid slurped an ice cream cone, and someone else chewed on a crisp apple. Everywhere was the sight of food, the smell of food, the sound of food. Everywhere were signs telling people how wonderful it was to eat. In windows and on billboards, in magazines and on TV the message was EAT! EAT! EAT!

Anguished, tortured with desire, sweating as he forced himself to resist the rumbling demands of his body for food, he thought what a cruel torment life really was. If you gave in to temptation, if you ate, gorging yourself on sweets and chocolate and all the goodies dangled temptingly before your eyes, then you were reprimanded by other signs, by articles and lectures on the evils of overeating, the horrors of fat, and the virtues of self-control, restraint, and skinniness. Thin people, you were told, were happier, healthier, and lived longer. It was a cruel world, a conspiracy of the thin against the fat. Unfair!

Why not a world where fat was praised and thinness disapproved? Where thin people were pointed out, laughed at, and told how ugly they were. *That* would be equal justice. Not that Marcus would inflict on skinny people what they had for so long inflicted on fat people. No, at heart he was a humanist. There would be no hypocrisy in his fat world, no telling people on the one hand to eat, and then condemning them for doing what they were told!

Marcus opened his eyes and saw a shining Brave New Fat World. Columbus Avenue, Food Center of the World, Fat Street of the United States of Plenitude, where the national symbol was the horn of plenty standing on top of a building: a two-story-high neon sign spilling out an endless river of sparkling goodness. People streamed in and out of the food stores. Everyone was eating, fat and cheerful. Eating was goodness and happiness. Eating was patriotic. It was the right and the duty of every person to eat more. That was the American way. We were a nation of producers and eaters. No other country in history had ever produced the goods and goodness that the United States of Goodness produced. The Fat Way was the patriotic way.

The skinny folk (unfortunately there would still be some of them left), the people who wouldn't fatten up, or who were resistant to fat mind therapy, or who had naturally sour, thin dispositions—they wouldn't be discriminated against and abused. Not in the U.S. of Plenitude. But, surrounded by so many contented fat people they'd naturally be hard to see. Storekeepers would serve them last, they'd mostly be overlooked at bus stops, and in restaurants they'd be lucky to get seats. Also, normal fat people would find skinny people distasteful to look at, so they'd have to work in backs of stores, in corners of offices, and do all the distasteful jobs in factories that made normal fat people lose their appetites.

Marcus got off the bus at Triangle Park, still dreaming about the Brave New Fat World. The fat, contented, peaceful new world.

"Hey, Rosen Balloon!"

Marcus blinked. Skinny Willis Pierce, that bag of bones, that dangerous, subversive element in the Brave New Fat World.

"Hey, Elephant Boy!"

Marcus shook his head. No discrimination in the Fat World, but the skinny ones would have to be watched closely. Skinny bodies sheltered thin, ill-nourished minds. Those who wouldn't fatten up, those dissatisfied bony elements might try to make everyone else as sick and as skinny as they were. If necessary the leaders of the Fat World would put all the skinny ones in special education classes where they could learn a more contented and pleasant way of thinking and living.

"Hey, Fat Horse, watch where you're going. You almost stepped on me. Are you deaf, Fat Man?"

Willis's voice was lost in the wind of Marcus's world where he was exploring the inner workings of the new Fat Educational System. Skinny people who weren't trainable, who didn't respond satisfactorily to fat mind therapy and appetite-enhancing classes (misfits probably existed even in the "perfect" society) would finally have to be picked up like dingy rats and flushed down the toilet . . .

FOUR

SALLY'S FRIEND Bill Brenner was back. "Your bald-headed boyfriend called," Marcus teased. "He's on his way over."

"Boyfriend!" Sally hated that expression. "It ought to be purged from the language. It's misleading and silly. He's not a boy, and he's much much more than a friend. Where'd he call from?"

"His apartment," Marcus said. He was eager to talk to Bill. For a long time he'd been thinking of asking Bill some questions about his father. But he didn't want to talk in front of his mother. Alone, Bill would give him straight answers. They joked and teased a lot, but when they were alone together, they could be serious, too.

Bill had just returned from a tour with the Famous Musical Company. Tokyo, Singapore, Warsaw, London. When Marcus thought of the cities of the world he thought of Bill. Bill, tall and slow, with his shiny balding head and the veins on his forehead popping as he played his trumpet. Bill who used to play "horsie" with the small Marcus, and who sent him stamps for his album from every country in the world. Bill, who had been everywhere, was back, sitting down to dinner with Marcus and Sally.

He wore a black turtle-neck shirt under a belted jacket and was smoking his pipe, producing a sweet, maple-scented cloud of smoke that hung over the table. He'd brought presents, as he always did, this time a wooden xylophone, gongs, and a handmade camel blanket for Marcus. That was a laugh.

"What am I supposed to do with this camel blanket?" Marcus said.

"Find a camel," Bill said.

His mother's laugh was rich and as melodious as a flute, high and then low and deep in her throat. "You're great, darling."

Marcus talked more than anyone, telling Bill how much his new football cost, and how much Rossi the butcher was paying for delivering on Friday nights. And how the neighborhood was changing, the old white-elephant mansions coming down all along East Broadway. And he told him the plans he'd made to lose weight.

That got a laugh from both Sally and Bill. Marcus had to laugh himself. With Bill back and all the excited talk, everything on the table looked too tempting—the fresh rolls, the butter, the roast lamb, the little mounds of green mint jelly, and the buttered carrots. When he wasn't talking, he was eating.

"You don't think we eat this way every day, do you, Bill? Around here we get it when we can." He looked slyly at his mother.

"Around here you get more than enough," Sally said, unperturbed. "Marcus hasn't talked this much since you left, Bill. I think he's been saving it all to tell you. He doesn't tell it to me. Lately he's mum as a mouse with Mom, isn't that so, Marcus? Well, we've both missed you, Bill. Just think, you've been all over while we've been sitting here like two sticks in the mud. I envy you the travel."

"Travel—you can have it," Bill said, dismissing the world with a disparaging wave of his hand. "It's like the Army, Sally. Join the Army and see the world. They say. But what you see is Army camps, Army vehicles, and Army types. It's the same with the musical company. You travel with music people, talk to music people, and what you see from your hotel room you could see better on a picture postcard. In other words, nothing."

"I've always wanted to travel," Sally said. "If we had been there, Marcus and I, we would have gotten a lot out of it."

"If you had been there—" Bill knocked his pipe against the side of a brass ashtray he'd brought to Sally years ago. "That would have changed everything. With you, I would have gotten out, gone around, seen things, talked to people. Alone, I don't talk to anyone. You should have come, Sally. I asked you to come. You could have."

"Oh, no, I couldn't," Sally said. "Give up my job? I have a family to care for."

"I have plenty of money," Bill said.

"Not my money," Sally retorted. "My job is my independence. I'll never take money from you or anyone else."

"You can give it all to me," Marcus said. "All gifts gratefully accepted." As much as to amuse, he said it to tease his mother, who was a fanatic about her independence. She was always refusing things from relatives. When his Grandmother May wanted to buy him a bicycle, Sally insisted that he earn half the money, and she flatly refused whenever Uncle Albert, who ran a shoe store, tried to give him free sneakers or shoes. Marcus assured Bill he didn't have Sally's scruples.

"Maybe if I'd sent you a dollar for every letter you promised me, I would have gotten some mail from you," Bill said. "I just didn't think money was the way to your heart."

"You know me—" Marcus made paws of his hands. "Doggie. I can't write letters."

"Correct that. Doggie *won't* write," Sally said. "I urged him to write. I said, 'Marcus, write, you don't have to write a masterpiece. Write whatever you feel like writing. Bill will enjoy anything.' "

"I didn't feel like writing anything," Marcus said.

"Are you disagreeing with me, Marcus?"

"Never, Sally!" He sank down in his chair and picked up the chair opposite with his feet. It wasn't that he hated writing letters so much. He'd often made up letters in his head as part of the stories he told himself about his father. But not to Bill. Bill he could tell everything to when he returned, and Marcus always did.

When Bill was ready to leave later in the evening, Marcus said he'd walk down to the bus stop with him. He had something to talk to Bill about.

"It's cold out," Sally said. "Why don't you talk here?"

"It's private," Marcus said. He stood outside in the

hall, waiting for them to say good night. Bill had his arm around Sally's waist. "By next week I'll have my apartment cleaned up, and you can come visit me," he said.

Sally patted his arm. "Call me at work tomorrow." Then to Marcus, "Don't be long. It's late."

Downstairs on the street the wind lifted paper and leaves, crackling the plastic sheeting on the new construction. Bill turned up his collar and pulled down his hat. Marcus dug his hands deep into his pockets.

"What weather!" Bill said. "I can taste winter coming. You sure you want to go all the way?"

"It's okay," Marcus said. He hunched his shoulders against the chill. He had been waiting for a long time to ask Bill about his father, but now that they were alone, he didn't know how to start.

"How's the situation in school?" Bill said as they crossed 273rd Street. "What're people griping about these days? Too much homework? Not enough student representation? Smoking rooms for students? That's always a hot issue."

Bill and his mother were alike in that they were both interested in politics and organizations, but Marcus didn't share that interest and he wasn't really paying attention as Bill talked about the organization-minded European students. He was trying to find exactly the right way to open up on the subject of his father. It was hard, even though it was usually easy to talk to Bill. He'd think of one thing to say, and that seemed wrong. Then he'd think of beginning another way, and that seemed just as wrong. Finally, he had to take a breath, grab the pig's tail, and say it.

"Bill, did you know my father?"

Bill turned to look carefully at Marcus. "No, I never knew him. What makes you ask?"

"You never met him? Or talked to him? Don't you know what he was like?"

Bill shook his head. "I only know the little bit Sally told me. What's this all about, Marcus? Why this sudden interest in your father?"

Marcus felt a tightening in his stomach. There was a question that he needed to have answered—a question that filled him with the fear that Bill would refuse to answer. He was ashamed that he even had to ask.

"Bill—do you know my father's name?" He felt that there was no power in his voice, as if his breath had been blown away. "Did my mother ever tell you my father's name?"

"You don't know it?" Bill acted surprised. "I told you I never met the man, and I never heard his name mentioned, either."

Marcus was sure he'd said everything wrong, and whatever Bill knew he'd hold back, because Sally didn't want Marcus to know about his father, and had told Bill not to tell him anything.

"Your mother doesn't talk about him to me," Bill said. "She never has. Why don't you ask her whatever you want to know?"

Marcus shook his head. "Sally never tells me anything about him." He was deep into the injustice of his life. His mother was everything to him—she was good, she was the best and the most beautiful person, and she treated him fairly, except when it came

44

to his father. She wouldn't tell Marcus one single thing about the unknown man who was his father. It wasn't right. It was unfair and painful. He had a right to know.

"Marcus, they broke up long before I came into the picture. All I know is that Sally wanted you from the beginning. And I have the impression that your father wasn't keen on having children. That's why your mother brought you up on her own—and did a damn fine job of it, too."

"If you don't know anything about him, how do you know my father didn't want children?" Marcus said.

Bill put his hand up to shield his face from the gusting wind. "You're right, Marcus. I don't definitely know even that. You ought to ask Sally, that would be the simplest thing. Ask your mother, I'm sure she'll tell you whatever you want to know."

No, that was the last thing he could do. That was why he was talking to Bill. His mother would think he was dissatisfied, or mad at her for something. If he told her all the times he'd thought and daydreamed about his father, she'd think he hated their life together. And nothing was farther from the truth.

Bill put his warm hand on the back of Marcus's neck. "Don't make too much of this, Marcus. Speak to your mother. Trust her. Sally doesn't hold back things. She's too straightforward, a really special person. You can believe anything she says."

Marcus listened, a hard knot in his stomach, waiting, wanting more, uncertain. Did Bill really know nothing about his father? Or was he afraid to tell him

45

and get Sally mad? Bill didn't say anything else, and Marcus was uncertain what to do next. He'd been eager to talk to Bill alone, sure that Bill would have at least some answers to the questions that had been building in him for weeks, for months. And now there was nothing.

As they approached the bus stop, a ragged man stepped out in front of them from the shadow of a building. He wore a limp baggy coat, his face was thin, his nose lumpy, his unkempt hair held in place by a black headband. "Brothers," he said, "I'm hungry and sick. Brothers—"

Marcus had been thinking so hard about his father that for a moment, startled, uncertain, he thought this beggar was his father returned.

The beggar blocked their path. "Brothers, can't you help a man when he's down? I've been sick." There was a sweet, pukey smell about him.

The tightness in Marcus's stomach went to his throat. He felt he would throw up. Could this man be his father? How could he tell? What if his father had been brought down by a powerful enemy and was wandering through the streets, weak and sick, searching for his son? In the fantasy that instantly flashed through his mind, he imagined himself stepping forward. *I am your son, Marcus Rosenbloom.*

My son! The man, startled, put out his hand, in his clouded eyes the light of recognition, and then pride. The rags fell away. The man straightened up. *My son! My own son! . . .*

Bill had produced a dollar and was handing it to the beggar. "Eat something first," he advised the man, who quickly turned away and disappeared. Bill put his arm through Marcus's. "Maybe he'll eat something, probably he'll drink it up. Still, it's hard to say no. I never say no because you never can tell. That man is down today, I might be down tomorrow. That's the way life is."

Marcus, looking up at Bill, thought that his father would have this understanding, too, to be able to give to a man in need. No, his father wasn't the beggar. He'd been mistaken. Just the opposite. His father was like Bill. He understood what life was like. He was generous and open-handed. His father carried pockets full of dollar bills for men down on their luck and was known by everyone. They called his father the Dollar Man. The kids came running when he appeared.

Dollar Man! Here comes the Dollar Man! You could always rely on the Dollar Man.

FIVE

O N HIS WAY to Miss Blesch's eighth-period English
class, Marcus caught a glimpse of Vivian in the
crowded corridor. He was only an arm's length away,
but she passed, not noticing him. She raised her hand
to greet someone else; the same warm friendly smile
she had for him, she had for everyone else. He saw the
flash of a ring on her little finger, a ring with two tiny
entwined gold hearts. The thought that some other
boy had given her that gold ring made him flush with
jealousy.

In English class he didn't hear anything Miss
Blesch was saying. He was making arrows and rock-
ets across the cover of his notebook and splashing
into stars on the inside pages. The arrows pointed to
the letter V twined with the letter M. He carried on
private conversations. Vivian, what a beautiful and
unusual name! Marcus was an unusual name, too.
Didn't she think so? What did she think it meant?

He thought about the dark hall in the McNutleys'
house, the grip of Vivian's long, clean-looking fingers.
He looked down at his own hands—stumpy, bitten-
down nails, hands made ugly with half-chewed-off
warts. Too nice to say anything, Vivian must surely

48

have been repelled by those hands. Could she really have meant all those things she said, or had she just been having fun with him?

Crack! There was a bullet-like report from the front of the room. A book slamming down on the desk. Miss Blesch was off on one of her rampages. "Wake up, you zombies!" She threw open the windows, letting icy blasts into the overheated room. "This class—" she said, with a shudder of disgust, "if I may be excused the misuse of the word. It's hard to think of you as a class in any sense. Unless it's a class in good slumber habits, but *there*, there's nothing I can teach you! Every member of this class is gifted to the utmost in the ability to sleep with his eyes open. The wakeful dead!"

Miss Blesch was sharp and tough. Despite the hour and her skepticism, she taught and the class learned. "The subject to be discussed today," she said, "is a possible theme for a class play. Who has anything to contribute?" She sat up on the edge of the desk, her knees crossed. Her knees were round and smooth, and Marcus could see the white of the bone under the skin. Was he being disloyal to Vivian by looking at Miss Blesch's knees? He didn't even know what Vivian's knees looked like, but he knew everything about Miss Blesch's knees.

Miss Blesch had a tiny fat face in each of her knees. There was even a little mouth in each face that moved. The way he was concentrating, Miss Blesch's voice was coming from her knees. "Mr. Rosenbloom—" The knees were talking to him.

"Mr. Rosenbloom!"

His head snapped up. "Miss Blesch—?"

"Thank you for joining us. We're honored. Now, what is your comment, Mr. Rosenbloom?"

He didn't have the foggiest notion what she was talking about. "I'm sorry—" His eyes were drawn irresistibly back to her knees. He couldn't shake the feeling that her cute fat knees were talking to him.

"Mr. Rosenbloom, do you know anything of what's been going on in this class? Where have you been, may I ask? Your mind—where is it? What are you thinking of?"

He tore his eyes away from her knees, did a little aimless dance with his fingers across the desk. "I'm sorry, Miss Blesch, I wasn't listening."

"We're talking about the class play, Mr. Rosenbloom. For the last time, what is your suggestion on the matter? You have given it thought, haven't you? That was the assignment."

"A class play—well, it should have many parts, with —uh—a lot of action, shootouts, and chases—"

"Oh, I see, you want us to put on a wild west show. What original thinking!"

"I nominate Marcus as the horse," Willis said.

"Shut up, Willis. Mr. Rosenbloom, give me the courtesy of looking at me when I speak to you." His eyes had again drifted to her knees. "Is this class so boring? Sit up, please!"

Miss Blesch had never come down so hard on Marcus before. He'd always thought he was one of her favorites, and he usually enjoyed her sarcasm and wit. But this wasn't one of his good days. Hot and embarrassed, he sat up so hard he banged his knees

50

into the bottom of his desk and sent his books and papers and pens flying. The class broke up, but not Miss Blesch.

"I want you back here after school, Mr. Rosenbloom," she said. "Your attitudes need some careful examination." Then she told the class to pipe down. "We've had enough comic relief for one period. This class makes me despair. All of you—shut up and turn around. Maybe we can salvage something from this so-called class period!" And she handed out yellow paper for an unannounced quiz on the work they should have prepared but hadn't.

When Marcus returned to Miss Blesch's room after the last bell the only person there was Flo Weaver, sitting up front and correcting papers. He'd seen Flo with Dorrity a couple of times, and she was in his English class, but he'd never talked to her before. He wanted to make a good impression on her. Maybe she'd mention him to Dorrity. He cleared his throat. "Where's Miss Blesch?"

"Having a smoke in the teachers' lounge. She'll be right back. You're supposed to wait."

"I know." He wandered idly up the aisles, conscious of Flo and the way her sweater was hiked up in back, showing white skin. Flo was one of those girls who already looked like a woman.

"What are you looking at?" she said, sitting up and stretching her plump arms over her head. He could only shake his head. His face was flaming. "I know," she said smugly. "I can always tell. So what's wrong with looking. Look all you want. I don't mind. You here for skipping class, too?"

"I fell asleep in class," he said. "Low criminal stuff."

She smiled. "Every time I skip, Miss Blesch makes me correct papers. That's no punishment. I like correcting papers. It's better than going home. But I'm getting tired of it now."

"Hand over some," Marcus said, sitting down next to her. "I'll help."

"Thanks," she said, giving him part of the stack. "You mark them with the stencil and I'll add them up. That way we'll get done faster."

Working together, they were done in fifteen minutes. "Great!" Flo said, gathering the papers and putting them on Miss Blesch's desk. "You were a good help, Marcus."

"Look," he said expansively, "you want to go. Why don't you go ahead? I'll tell Miss Blesch you were here and finished your work."

"Sure, and she'll get me for skipping out on her and call my father. That will be the end of me. My father will beat me silly."

"Your father hits you?" He couldn't keep the surprise from his voice.

"Doesn't yours?" Before he could say yes or no, she pulled up the legs of her jeans to show him the purplish welts. "He did that with a belt," she said almost proudly. "Once he gets going, he doesn't care which end he uses."

"Why does he do it?" Marcus said, staring at the purple welts.

Flo shrugged. "He can hit for no reason. If he just thinks I'm not listening to him, or he doesn't like the way I look at him or answer him back. I don't know, I can't figure him out. He's crazy. He says I have to do exactly what he says. Fat chance! Why should I? He does what he pleases, and so do I! Does your father pound you a lot? Or are you too big for him? It's easier for boys, they're bigger and they can hit back."

"It's just me and my mother," he said.

"Oh, your mother's divorced? So is Jim Dorrity's. You know Jim Dorrity?"

"Yes," he said eagerly. "Sure. I've seen him around a lot." He would have liked to go on talking about Dorrity, but Flo went back to her family.

"My mother couldn't stand my father. She walked out on him, moved away. Only she left me behind to take care of him. And now I'm stuck!"

"You really don't like him?" Marcus asked.

"Mothers are better," Flo said with conviction. "I wish I was with my mother instead of my father. I really do. Does your mother have a guy?"

"She has an old friend," Marcus said. "I don't mean he's *old*. Bill plays the trumpet, I mean for a living."

"Weird," Flo said. She went to the door and looked down the hall. "We go to my father's girl friend's house in Trumball Park every week. She has it all decorated in French Provincial style. Everything's so beautiful, and matches perfectly. Even the piano is French Provincial. I can play the piano a little. Do you play a musical instrument?"

"I play the hi-fi." Stupid! Why did he make such a stupid remark? And to make it worse, he had to show her how he turned the knobs, rotating both hands the

53

way guys did when they were talking about girls'
breasts. She must think he was an idiot. *That's* what
she'd tell Dorrity about him.

"I never see my father," he said, trying to regain
lost ground. "If I saw him on the street, I wouldn't
recognize him."

"You wouldn't recognize your own father? Come
on, cut it out, Marcus. Where does he live?"

"Well, he's—I really can't tell you."

She looked at him sharply. "Are you bulling me or
something? What is he, a jailbird?"

"No!"

She cocked her head, shaking a finger at him. "The
way you say that, Marcus—" She gave him a knowing
look. "Listen, don't be ashamed. Once my father
got arrested for drinking, and another time he started
a fight with a cop. Both times they threw him in jail.
So what about your father? You can tell me."

He looked squarely into her eyes, already hearing
an inner voice like a character in a TV spy drama. *I'm
not at liberty to divulge any information . . .*

The Bureau Chief of Secrets was beckoning him
from behind his desk. "Follow me and ask no questions." The Chief swiveled in his chair, revealing a
trapdoor on the floor of the office, opening onto narrow stairs that led through a dimly lit tunnel to a
hidden room under the building. There Marcus was
met by his father wearing a trench coat and a big
State Trooper's hat over his rough, creased face that
showed the marks of weather and hard experience.
There was a crooked white scar on his father's forehead, and below his mouth another scar as if a flap of

skin had been sliced through and then laid loosely back over his chin. His father didn't talk about his injuries. "You do what you have to do," his father said sternly. "Working for the government demands a lot from a man. Your loyalty has to be to your Commander in Chief and your country first, and then to your family. You understand, Marcus?" He put a big hand on Marcus's shoulder. "I'm off on a secret mission that will keep me under wraps for several years. You're the only person outside my Chief who knows about it. Not a word must ever escape your lips!"

Marcus stood tall. "You can count on me, sir!"

"I've always known that," his father said . . .

Flo peered into his face. "Marcus, why are you looking so funny? You're standing stiff as a board."

Marcus became aware of the way his hands were clamped at his sides, his shoulders stiffly back. He slumped against a desk, and put his hands casually in his pockets. "Practicing improving my posture. Special exercises—"

Flo was no longer listening. "Jimmy!" she exclaimed, turning. Dorrity had suddenly appeared in the doorway, hands hooked in his belt, sandy hair over his collar. Behind him, Phillips and Bisner peered coolly at Marcus. But Marcus felt only Dorrity's glance, with that slow secret smile, as if he'd just stepped out of Marcus's head and knew exactly what Marcus was thinking. It was startling and uncanny. Dorrity, as tall as he, with that white scar splitting his eyebrow, seemed to be talking to Marcus with his eyes over the heads of the others. There was sympathy and understanding in his glance, as if he were saying, *That's tough about your father being away* . . .

Your father, too . . . Marcus's face expressed his own understanding.

Dorrity's eyes that could read the unspoken secrets in Marcus's mind spoke to him. *We have a lot in common. We should be friends* . . .

"This is Marcus, everybody," Flo was saying, introducing him to the others.

"What's he in detention for?" Bisner pushed into the room and began chalking a squat gnomish figure on the blackboard. "I bet he's the teacher's pet."

"You're wrong, he's a real bad boy," Flo said, giving Marcus a conspiratorial look. "He tells all the teachers where to get off, don't you, Marcus? He's Mr. Trouble to everyone around here."

Glancing at Dorrity, Marcus gladly acknowledged his ill repute.

"What is this, a club meeting?" Miss Blesch had returned. "Clean off that blackboard!" She took the chalk from Bisner's hand. "School is over. What are you three boys doing here? Don't tell me detention is becoming fashionable."

Unabashed, Phillips grinned at Miss Blesch. "You're cute, Miss Blesch."

Dorrity had taken a seat near the door. "We're just waiting for our friends."

Marcus looked up. Did Dorrity mean him, too?

Miss Blesch kept Flo only a minute afterward, glancing at the corrected papers, then lecturing her briefly about skipping class before dismissing her. All three boys left with her. Marcus looked after them with a sinking feeling.

"Can I go, too, Miss Blesch?" If she released him now he could still catch up to them.

But Miss Blesch made him wait. "I've something to talk to you about, Marcus." She sat down in one of the student desks and told him to sit down next to her. "Now, Marcus, you're one of my better pupils. What happened to you today? It's not like you to be so dim. I hate to see the few that are responding to my class sinking to the level of the others. I count on you few. If you continue to let me down, Marcus, this class won't be worth teaching." She was not at all sarcastic.

"I'm sorry, Miss Blesch." It was hard for him to pay attention. His eyes kept going to the door. He promised not to fall asleep again in class, he promised to give his best, he was ready to promise anything so she'd stop talking and he could get away and find Dorrity again.

Dorrity. Marcus hadn't found him after school and now he'd gone out again after supper to search the edge of the Shopping Plaza. It was cold out, and most of the stores were shut. People hurried by. Nobody was near the fountain. Disappointed, Marcus jumped up onto the concrete rim, moving around the circumference as fast as he could. Then he turned and went completely around the other way. The revolving red spotlight in the center of the empty fountain scattered tall black shadows on store windows and the bright-dark faces of hurrying passers-by.

He dropped off the cement ring and sat on the

bench where he'd seen Dorrity sit the other night. The fountain spotlight kept flicking across his eyes, blurring his vision. Dorrity. He'd never felt this drawn to anyone before. Dorrity with his open face, those inscrutable eyes, and the white scar where his eyebrow was split. Almost as he'd imagined his father's scarred face. The two faces, his father's and Dorrity's, mingled in his mind, till they were one.

Dorrity was open, but he had secrets, too. He knew whatever it was that a fellow had to know in the world. Nothing shook Dorrity. He could probably do anything, get anything he wanted. If Marcus could be like Dorrity—if he could feel that control and mastery and confidence in the world . . .

Marcus lay on the bench and looked up through the bare trees to the pink Kosher Hot Dog sign that lit up the sky above a nearby building. The wind nipped at his skin where his shirt was pulled out. It was cold all right, so cold that almost everybody was indoors, but Marcus felt relaxed and comfortable. Rugged really. Most people couldn't stand the weather this way. Marcus, too, needed to stay outside and on the street more. He ought to be out in all kinds of weather, gradually building up his resistance to cold and wet. If he could sleep out here on bare wood, he could sleep anywhere.

He'd read once about a guy living in a big packing case on the roof of a building. All he'd had was this packing case and a sleeping bag. Marcus could do that, too. If it got too bitter cold in winter he'd find a cellar somewhere. Food wouldn't be a problem. He'd just buy food when he was really hungry. Maybe once a day. If he didn't have food around all the time he'd be sure to lose weight.

That would be the life. Independent. Not having to think about anyone but himself. Doing what he wanted when he wanted. He'd work just enough to get by, and for the rest of the time he'd wander around and see what was going on in the world. He imagined himself sitting on a bench like this in another city, with his arms up on the back the way Dorrity did. Maybe he and Dorrity would travel together. The thought of Dorrity made him look toward the laundromat at the end of a long line of stores. He'd once seen Dorrity and the others in there. He turned up his collar and started toward the laundromat, putting one foot in front of the other, Indian style. A couple crossed his path and he followed them at a distance, keeping them in sight, moving silently . . .

Little Bear with his father, Running Bear, moved silently, swiftly, through the forest. Suddenly Running Bear veered to one side of the path and flattened himself against the ground. Little Bear froze. Then he crept up to join his father. Below, in a little valley, a group of frightened palefaces were crashing through thick growths of bushes and fallen trees. They had lost the path and were wandering blindly through the forest.

When, moments later, Running Bear and Little Bear showed themselves, the palefaces were struck dumb with amazement. They didn't know there were still Indians in this part of the country. Where did they come from? Were they real Indians? Would they teach the palefaces their wisdom?

Running Bear tired of their incessant talk and held up his hand for silence. He told them his son would show them the way out of the forest, then he disappeared as silently as he'd appeared. Little Bear led the way to the trail that led to the river. The strangers were amazed and grateful and wanted to know how they could find Little Bear again. They wanted to reward him for saving their lives, but Little Bear, after pointing the way across the river, disappeared into the forest to join his waiting father . . .

A truck rumbled past Marcus. He crossed the street and stared into the brightly lit laundromat. A woman wearing a quilted green jacket and a pink kerchief was folding towels. Two children were reading comics in a corner. Dorrity wasn't there.

Disappointed, Marcus crossed East Broadway and then picked his way across the torn-up ground where the overhead expressway was being built. The concrete arches were up and in place, waiting like unfinished monuments. In the unsettling dark, the wind whistled around the concrete piers.

Marcus stood across the street from the McNutley apartment, looking at their windows. The curtains were drawn in front, but there was light inside and he could see shadows. He imagined that Vivian would come outside and be threatened by a mugger, but he'd be right there to save her. He'd drive off the criminal with a sudden and unexpected charge. He heard Vivian's grateful outcry, "Marcus, you're wonderful!"

Several times he crossed the street, going straight and boldly to the McNutleys' door as if he were going to ring the bell. Vivian would answer, of course, but what if her father was standing directly behind her? Marcus crossed back to stand in the shadow of the trees. Shadowy figures—he felt their presence everywhere. In the long, crooked arms of trees hovering over him, in the noisy leaves and papers trapped against buildings and fences, in the blank unlit sides of buildings. It was late and cold. He felt the presence of shadows, indistinct faces, and inarticulate voices. He strained to hear. There was a message out there. He felt on the edge of something, some knowledge, something he'd never known before. He remembered the amazing and uncanny look he and Dorrity had exchanged earlier that day.

And then he remembered that he hadn't found Dorrity, not after school, not in these cold dark hours.

He thought of the dreams of his father. And then the sinking dark ache of his loneliness.

He ran home, crossing lighted corners and running down one long black street after another. He was an idiot, standing outside in the freezing night and making up stories to warm himself. All those stories to make himself feel good, stories about Vivian and Dorrity, and that stupid dream about someday meeting his father. It was never going to happen. He didn't know where his father was, or what he did, or even who he was or what he was like. He might have

61

passed his father a hundred times or a thousand times on these very streets, and never known it. And if he ever did meet him, his father would look at him, and he wouldn't even know him. *Marcus Rosenbloom*, he'd say. *Who are you?*

SIX

MARCUS WAITED for Bernie after school in front of the building. One . . . two . . . three . . . four . . . at the count of fifty he was off, cutting diagonally across an empty lot, stopping home long enough to swallow a glass of milk and get his pigskin, then heading straight for the green adjoining the highway on East Broadway. He'd seen Dorrity's gang there a couple of times playing touch football on the grass where the signs read NO BALL PLAYING.

Just as he'd hoped, they were there, leaning against the parked cars at the edge of the green. He saw Dorrity first, sitting up on a car fender with Flo leaning against him, her jeans embroidered with squirrels and chipmunks, little animals with big eyes. Marcus approached hesitantly. He didn't know how he would be greeted, or if he would be greeted at all. Did they want him to hang around? Or would they, when he reached them, suddenly get up and move off, leaving him standing there?

It was Flo who recognized him first. "There's Mr. Trouble," she said, waving to him.

Phillips' sharp-eyed smile wasn't reassuring. "Marcus, the Rose in Bloom, how does your garden grow? What kind of rose are you, Rose in Bloom?"

Marcus's eyes went to Dorrity. "I'm a wild rose."

Bisner, in a cut-off black sweat shirt, acted as if Marcus didn't exist, staring woodenly at the passing traffic.

"Rosenbloom." Dorrity held up two fingers, calling for Marcus's football. Marcus, hot to the roots of his hair, lateraled it to Dorrity, who examined the label, fingered the lacing, and sniffed the leather.

"It's not plastic," Marcus said.

Dorrity nodded. "The real thing." He held the ball in one hand, twirling it, tossing it up in the air.

"Where'd you steal it, Rosenbloom?" Bisner sneered. He never seemed to have anything good to say to Marcus.

"I didn't steal it, I bought it."

"I bet."

Marcus reacted defensively. "I did buy it. My mother paid half, and I paid the rest."

Dorrity lateraled the ball back to Marcus, who was sure he'd said absolutely the wrong thing, mentioning his mother. Reminding them how young he was. Younger than all of them.

"You've got a good-looking mother," Phillips said. "She's so good-looking I didn't even think she looked like a mother."

"What do you mean?" Bisner seemed intent on disagreeing with everything said. "If she's his mother then she looks like his mother."

Phillips listened to Bisner impassively. "I thought she was his sister, okay?" Continuing, he recited in comic fashion, "Who was that woman I saw you with

64

last night? That was no woman, that was my mother!"
Phillips held up his arms. "Did all you perverts hear
that? Why aren't you all going yuk, yuk, yuk!"

"Yuk!" Flo obliged.

"Thank you," Phillips said. "When I saw young
Rosenbloom and his mother going along arm in arm,
it gave me a start. You don't see that kind of devotion
anymore. Young Rosenbloom and his mother have to
be something special. When's the last time you were
arm in arm with your mother, Dorrity?"

Dorrity, who was staring moodily off into space,
said, "My mother and I don't touch."

Phillips nodded sagely. "Exactly. The last time my
mother put her arm around me like that she was trying to pick my pocket."

"Come off it," Flo said. "Where do you get that
stuff? Your mother is all right. She always has a nice
way about her, something nice to say to me. There's
nothing wrong with your mother."

"If you were nicer to your mother, she'd be nicer
to you," Bisner added.

Phillips looked dismally at Bisner. "She probably
wishes I was like you and followed her around like a
dumb dog. Arf, arf! Here, Poochie, here's your bone!"

Bisner made a threatening gesture. "Who you calling a dumb dog?"

Phillips ducked, but kept up the teasing. "Here,
doggie—smart doggie—here's a nice little bone."

Bisner faced one, and then another. They were all
laughing, but instead of turning on Phillips again, he
went after Marcus. "What are you laughing at?" he

demanded. He was older and stronger than Marcus, and there was an aggressiveness and readiness to use his fists that made Marcus uneasy.

Marcus couldn't shake a nervous smile from his face. He looked over at Dorrity who was watching with a disinterested expression.

"Wipe that smile off your fat face before I wipe it off for you," Bisner ordered.

Marcus looked at Dorrity again. He didn't want to back down in front of him. "Why, who are you?" he said to Bisner.

"I told you—wipe it!"

"I can smile if I want to, all day long if I like." And to prove it he smiled at Bisner, who was now leaning so close to Marcus that he could see the pores and blackheads in Bisner's forehead. Nose to nose. Staring each other down. Any moment Marcus expected Bisner to hit him. He wanted to push Bisner's face away, but instead he kept his face close, not letting himself be intimidated.

"Leave the kid alone," Dorrity said. "He didn't do anything to you."

"Oh, yeah!" Bisner said, but he was the first to look away. Dorrity was laughing at him, and so were the others.

"Every time you open your mouth," Dorrity said, "you are stupid."

Bisner popped Marcus's football from under his arm and turned away.

Marcus retrieved the ball. He felt good. He hadn't backed off, and Dorrity had stood up for him.

Bisner, however, hadn't given up trying to get at

somebody, and he saw another chance when Flo's friend Barbara Michel appeared in jeans and a brown velour pullover. A swift, agile girl, she was ready to play at once. "Football! Let's play football," she said.

Marcus tossed her the ball and she tossed it to Dorrity.

"Hey, Barb," Bisner said slyly, "we've got someone new here who's dying to know you." He shoved Marcus toward the girl. "Meet Rosey Rosenbloom. He really goes for you. If I told you what this kid said he wants to do with you, you wouldn't believe it."

Barbara Michel looked at Marcus coldly. "I never said anything," he said. "He's making it up."

"No kidding, Barb," Bisner said. "Are you ready?"

Barbara went after Bisner, her fists clenched. Bisner, laughing, pushed Marcus between himself and Barbara, ducking away every time she swung at him.

Dorrity called a halt to the horseplay by announcing the game. "Touch football. I pick Barbara and Rosey for my team, the Reds." Flo, Bisner, and Phillips were the Whites. Marcus was in heaven, dreaming that he was carrying the ball, running, sliding, patterning from one side of the field to the other, slick as a fish, fast, strong, he and Dorrity too strong a team to be held down.

The three of them huddled together, their arms around each other. Barbara, cool ivory skin, on one side, and Dorrity, sandy yellow hair, on the other. "Rosey centers the ball, flips to Barb, who then flips to me."

Marcus faced the others across the scrimmage line.

Phillips bared his yellow teeth. Flo looked at him with narrowed eyes and Bisner threatened to walk over him.

"Hike," Barbara called. Excited and happy, nervous and sweaty, Marcus flipped the ball badly.

"Too high!" Barbara yelled. "You fat dumbbell." She could barely get the ball before the others were coming across the field toward her. She threw the ball wildly a moment before they tagged her. Phillips intercepted and scored a touchdown for the Whites.

"Butterfingers," Flo yelled. "Blubberpots. We'll cream you."

Marcus was ashamed to meet Dorrity's eyes. Barbara didn't spare him, either. "It was his fault, the fat nitwit. He threw the ball a mile over my head. Does he even know how to hold a ball?"

"Take it easy," Dorrity said. "He's going to do better this time." He patted Marcus on the butt. This time he'd center the ball to Marcus, and he and Barb would go to opposite sides as receivers. "Hit whoever's open," Dorrity said. "Just give us one of those long bullet passes."

Marcus pushed the hair from his eyes. Dorrity was in front of him now. Marcus looked over the line to the others waiting on their hands and knees, snarling and straining to get at him. He had to do better this time.

Dorrity clapped his hands. "Let's go. Let's mow them down!" They were in their line-up, two in front and one in back. Marcus looked around. There were people watching along the line of cars. Suddenly he thought he saw Bernie and that made him so nervous and uneasy he forgot what he had to do.

He saw them rushing him. He had the ball. He fell back, looking for his teammates, but it was too late. The others were nearly on top of him. He ran the ball to the sidelines as fast as he could, then changing direction he got over the line of scrimmage and down the field before he was hit from behind. Bisner caught him behind the knees and down he went. "Down like a bag of shit," Bisner yelled, but he couldn't knock the ball away from Marcus.

"Good boy!" Dorrity's pale eyes shone. "The same play," he said. This time they were going all the way.

Marcus found himself with the ball again, alone with the other side charging toward him. He saw Dorrity and then Barbara with her hands in the air far down the field. Marcus flung the ball. It was a beautiful smooth throw, the ball twirling, coming down perfectly. Barbara grabbed it and ran the rest of the way to the trees that marked the goal.

They played late into the afternoon. The sun was down behind the hospital and cold shadows fell across the field. The rush-hour cars were beginning to back up on East Broadway when they stopped. Marcus was hot and sweaty, he'd scraped his elbow, and both knees were muddy. But he felt great. He'd been accepted. He'd played good ball. He was sure Dorrity liked him, and Flo, too, and once they'd won, Barbara as well. Phillips, yes, and even Bisner, who had tried to get at him all afternoon; he felt they all accepted him now.

At home his mother was waiting for him. She was dressed to go out. "Where were you, Marcus? I was starting to get worried. We're going to see a movie. Say hello to Bill, he's in the living room."

Marcus pushed his shirt into his pants. He stood at the living-room entrance. "Hello, Bill." His cheeks were burning from the outdoors.

"You look like you've been engaged in the all-American sport," Bill said.

In the bathroom Marcus took off his muddy clothes. Then he washed his face and hands, splashing water over his head, and looking at himself in the mirror, at his tight red cheeks and the hair over his eyes.

Here! Here! He saw Dorrity running down the field, long sandy hair streaming. *Throw it, Marcus!—* reaching up for the ball. Dorrity liked him; he knew it was so.

Marcus bared his teeth, rolling up his lip and narrowing his eyes. He felt mean and tough and somehow older. He snarled at himself, flicking his fist at his face in the mirror. What control! What speed! He'd really played ball today.

The phone rang before he sat down to eat. "Marcus, take that," his mother said. "We're on our way out. That's probably Bernie. He called twice already."

Marcus took the phone from the kitchen counter and around the corner into the hall. "Hello, Rosenbloom residence."

"Where were you?" Bernie's voice was demanding and accusing, hurt and suspicious. "Where were you, anyway? I waited for you till three-thirty. Where'd you go?"

70

"I waited," Marcus said. "Where were you?"

"You didn't wait ten seconds," Bernie said.

"Oh, yes I did! You weren't there."

"I was there," Bernie said heatedly. "Where'd you go, anyway?"

"I was playing touch football, with Dorrity and the others."

"You're a fink, you know that?"

"Okay, so I'm a fink. If that makes you happy, say it."

"Why are you hanging around with those creeps? I don't like any of them. I don't like Dorrity, and I don't like stupid Bisner, and I don't like Phillips. He's so sarcastic. He thinks he's smarter than anyone else."

"You don't even know them, so what are you talking about?"

"Who wants to know them," Bernie said. "A bunch of stuck-up snobs."

Marcus was silent. Bernie was just blowing off steam.

"Besides, they're into drugs. Anybody that has any brains knows enough to stay away from creeps like that."

"Anything else?" Marcus said coolly. "Somebody's waiting for me."

"Okay! Good-by, idiot." And Bernie hung up.

SEVEN

"**O**KAY," HIS GRANDMOTHER SAID, "shoot, but it better not be questions about schoolwork. What I ever knew then I've forgotten long ago. And no riddles."

Marcus had come to his grandmother's to talk about his father. It had been in the back of his mind to talk to her ever since the night he'd tried and gotten nothing from Bill. His grandmother wasn't like Bill. She knew about everything and everyone from the beginning. Besides he'd never known her not to answer his questions.

They were in the kitchen of her Lanark Hill Road apartment. She was wearing tight black pants and gold slippers and a loose white shirt. Marcus liked everything about his grandmother—the way she looked and dressed—but she was self-conscious about her weight. "The original Mrs. Five-by-Five," she complained. "How's Sally? I spoke to her the other day and she invited me to a party she's making."

"It's for Bill," Marcus said. "A week from Saturday."

His grandmother moved rapidly, opening and closing the refrigerator and cupboard doors, then slicing carrots, tomatoes, and green peppers. A loaf of white bread lay on the counter. "Want something to eat, Markey? I'm glad you came by. I need company to help me eat this rabbit food. I swear I hardly eat and I still gain weight." She paused and counted off all the foods she didn't eat. "Butter, cream, ice cream, fatty meats, cakes, desserts. Everything that's good I don't eat, and I still gain weight."

He wanted to talk about his father, but she hardly gave him an opening. His grandmother was lively and funny, and she loved company, but once she started talking it was hard to get her to change directions. So he came out with it bluntly and plainly because he didn't want to talk about a million other things first.

"Grandma, do you remember my father?" He had positioned himself with his back against the wall. He wanted it to be matter-of-fact. A matter-of-fact question, and then some matter-of-fact answers.

His grandmother, however, reacted dramatically. She made an awful face and then spit in the sink. "You'll have to excuse me," she apologized. "That was a gut reaction. Next time warn me when you bring up certain subjects—like your father. What are you trying to do, Markey, ruin my supper?"

He waited, not speaking, shifting slowly from foot to foot, almost holding his breath, waiting for her to go on. But instead she went back to talking about her diet. "How am I going to lose weight, Markey?"

"I'm the wrong one to ask, Grandma." Then somehow he let himself be drawn into a discussion of food and diet, a subject he'd thought about a lot himself. "If you stick to a diet you'll lose weight," he said.

"That's my trouble. No will power. I get tempted and then I can't stop eating."

"Go on, you're perfect. If you come over every day, we'll diet together." She laughed. "Do you remember the concoctions I used to come up with before I went on this dopey diet? Waffles and ice cream, chocolate pudding and whipped cream. How about whipped cream on chocolate ice cream. My favorite! Doesn't it make you drool with desire?"

"Grandma, remember the question I asked you?"

His grandmother dismissed the question with a wave of her hand. "Not now, Markey. After I eat. I'd rather hear one of your dopey riddles now."

He'd stopped telling riddles years ago, but he indulged his grandmother. "I have two coins in my hand and they add up to fifty-five cents. One is not a nickel. What are they?"

"One's a fifty-cent piece, and one's a nickel! I remember all your dopey riddles, Markey," she said with satisfaction. And she went back to talking about food and the way people nowadays talked about nothing except what they ate, or didn't eat. "It doesn't make any difference, the things they tell you they put in their mouths—those liquid diets—" She drew down her lips in a grimace. "I'd rather die than eat some of that garbage they put in their mouths in the name of losing weight. It only proves that people love to torture themselves. That's what I tell them at work. You should hear them protest. Diet is what the doctor ordered, they say. Take this pill and don't eat that and you're not supposed to smoke. Like they're babies, instead of grown people."

"But smoking isn't good for you," Marcus said. "I wish you'd stop smoking, Grandma. It shortens your life."

"Talk about life," she said, off on another tack. "Do you remember the freight elevator man in my building? Little Frankie, that little man with that beautiful head of hair? A sweet little man—"

"Who?" Marcus said. He was thinking about his father. His father was the man he wanted to talk about. That was why he was here. "Grandma, I want to talk about my father."

"What's the matter with you, Markey? I'm talking about Frankie, the elevator man. He always asked after you. Don't you remember him?"

"Sure, Grandma."

"Well, he's gone."

"Gone?" Marcus said, interested despite himself.

"Dead. He died just like that." She snapped her fingers. "Dropped over dead. Never even went into the hospital. From his house straight into the funeral parlor. It was a tragedy, but if you have to go, the way he went is the best way—nonstop. Without all that delay and suffering of hospital and bawling relatives, and being jabbed with needles, and probes and pipes stuck in you where nobody has a right to go. So now do you remember Frankie?"

"Of course I do, Grandma." Frankie was the first person they would meet whenever he went with his grandmother to the factory loft where she worked. "My grandson, Marcus Rosenbloom," his grandmother would say each time. When Marcus was a little boy Frankie would give him a bow and then smile, showing

75

a gold tooth. "He is almost as good-looking as you, May."

"Better looking. Don't insult the boy."

Then on the floor of Shapiro's Dress Creations he had to first go with her to the glassed-in office where she showed him off to the boss, Mr. Shapiro himself. "I want you to see there are some things, Shapiro, that are more important than money."

Mr. Shapiro, in his shirt sleeves, looked hurt. "Did I say otherwise?"

On the floor everyone knew his grandmother and wanted her to come over. "May, May," the women called, looking up from their sewing machines. "Over here." They all wanted to see May's grandson, pinch his cheeks, holding him while they searched for candy or money in their pocketbooks. "He's so juicy, May. He's good enough to eat."

"Didn't I tell you?" she said. "This is my grandson, Marcus Rosenbloom. In our family we're all like movie stars . . ."

"So you remember that, Markey?"

"I remember a lot of things, Grandma. Do you remember things?"

"Too much," she said.

"Well—what about my father?"

She sighed and told him to get her a fresh pack of cigarettes from the top of the refrigerator. "I hide them now, like an alcoholic." He got the cigarettes and handed them to her. She lit one, put the pack down on the counter. "A man who looks at a family as a burden is not much of a man in my book, but Sally didn't look ahead. I tried to warn her. An unmarried woman with a child doesn't have an easy life. She let him go too easy. You were his son, too. He should have shared the responsibility and he should have been made to stay around. What boy doesn't need his father?"

He waited, his thirst for information barely slaked. "What was he like, Grandma? Tell me—what was his name? I don't know anything."

His grandmother sniffed the bread, then wrapped it. "Stale. Everything goes stale around here, it stays so long."

"Grandma, I don't want to talk about food."

"Oh, Markey, I know plenty, but if I told you anything it would be behind your mother's back, and she'd be so mad at me she wouldn't talk to me for the rest of my life. At my age, I can't risk that, Markey."

He begged her to tell him. "Grandma, I'm old enough to know things. I'm not a baby, I don't need Sally's permission for everything. Please, Grandma."

His grandmother had sat down and was looking around the room with a dissatisfied expression on her face. "Stale, this room's stale, too. I'm going to paint this kitchen a brighter color. It's like the inside of a closet in here. When I get ready to paint, will you come and help me, Markey?"

"You know I will. Please, Grandma, just tell me his name."

She looked at the wall, rolling the cigarette absently between her fingers. For a few moments he thought she really was going to tell him. This was his own precious little grandmother. "Grandma—"

Her hands lay limp in her lap. "It kills me to say no to you, Markey, but I can't do it behind Sally's back. I know how she feels about him."

"Nothing?"

She shook her head.

He was so disappointed he couldn't speak. The smoke from her cigarette curled gently upward. The ceiling seemed to press down on him, and the walls were like a closed box. A tight feeling clogged his throat, and tears stung his eyes. He was afraid he would cry in front of his grandmother. He couldn't hide the disappointment he felt. "Grandma, won't you tell me just one little thing?"

She put out her cigarette. "I just might have a picture of your father. Did you ever see his picture? She can't get mad at me for showing you that, if I can even find it."

He didn't dare speak. The idea of a picture was beyond anything he had expected. She dragged a chair to the closet and stood on it. "Your father was a good-looking guy, I'll say that for him. You take after your father when it comes to looks, although the Rosenblooms aren't so bad either. Your father was tall, just as tall as you're going to be, but you're better looking and a nicer person in every way than he ever was."

Marcus followed her while she searched the top shelves of several closets, sorting through shoeboxes and old round candy tins, pausing to look at yellowed pictures that she said she should have put into albums years ago. "I don't know—I thought I had it," she said. "Maybe I threw it out."

"Try some more, Grandma," he urged.

"For you, Markey." She pushed aside a bunch of stuff and found another shoebox full of pictures, then with a triumphant cry she held up a small photo.

"I remembered right," she said, handing Marcus the photo which showed a man behind the wheel of a massive black and chrome car of the 1950's.

That was his father at the wheel.

His grandmother looked over his shoulder, apologizing. "I thought it was a better picture than that. It's a beautiful picture of the car, though." The man's face was in shadow, nearly indistinguishable. "Your father had your grandfather take the picture. He wanted everyone to see him in that expensive car. Showing off. He was poor and buying that car made him feel rich. He was always getting around people who had more than he had. He hated being poor. I doubt if he's poor anymore."

Marcus looked at the picture carefully, holding it up to the light. He could barely make out all his father's features, but it was his father. Now at last he knew something! How proud his father had been of his car. The cocky way he had his elbow out the window, and not smiling at the camera. His father was the kind of man who didn't go around smiling all the time just because someone was taking his picture.

"I'll keep this, Grandma," he said, putting the photo in his breast pocket. It was more than he'd hoped for from the visit.

She put out her hand. "Oh, no, Markey, I just gave it to you to look at."

He backed away. He couldn't give it up. "I promise I won't let Sally see it." He held the picture over his head. He had to keep his grandmother off with one hand. "Grandma, don't, I promise. Sally won't see it. I'll hide it. She never goes in my stuff."

His grandmother got tired of chasing him. "If Sally finds it," she warned, "I'm not going to know anything about it, Markey."

Later, sitting on the bus, he took out the picture again, straightening it—it was already creased—holding it up to the light and examining it till he knew every inch of its surface. Meager as the photo was, it was the first really tangible link he had to his father. It proved that his father was real. He was more than the dream in Marcus's head.

Each time he looked at the photo, smoothing it and carefully holding it to the light, he felt hungrier for more knowledge about his father. The man in the picture had his collar open, his sleeves rolled up. He was free and easy and he drove big fast cars. Marcus brought the photo close to his eyes, wanting to magnify it, studying it minutely, trying to see into the shadows and beyond the limits of the picture. The desire to see, to know more about his father was like an ache inside him that would burn a hole through his body if it went unsatisfied.

EIGHT

THE SATURDAY of Sally's party for Bill, she kept
Marcus close to home all day. There were errands
to run. She sent him out for rye bread and seeded
rolls, and he had to carry up beer and soda, which he
put into the refrigerator. They pushed the dining
room table against the wall, put in both extension
leaves, and covered it with a starched white cloth. He
helped his mother carry out the food. Platters of sliced
delicatessen meats, cheeses, pretzels, potato salad,
pickles, two pounds of sliced rye bread and dark
pumpernickel, and a gorgeous glazed chocolate cake.

When it was nearly time for the guests to arrive,
Sally made him change his clothes and put on a
white shirt and a pair of clean jeans and shoes instead
of sneakers. His mother wore a long blue gown with a
square neck and a strong geometrical design embroidered along the edge. Her hair was combed out
and her eyes outlined with thick black lines.

Marcus helped himself to a handful of pretzels
from a bowl and then said, "Why don't I ever see my
father? Why doesn't he come to see me? You know
where he is, don't you!" He surprised himself with the
sudden, demanding way he'd spoken. Ever since he'd

seen his grandmother the week before he knew he was going to speak to his mother, but he didn't know it was going to come out in this aggressive way.

His mother turned and looked at him. "Well! Where did that come from?"

"Why? What's so surprising? I just want to know about my father."

"Out of the blue, this way?"

"It's not out of the blue. I talked to Bill, I talked to Grandma. Nobody will tell me anything."

"You don't have to talk to anyone else. I'll tell you," she said emphatically. "Why didn't you come to me first? Marcus, I haven't seen your father since before you were born. You know that. And I don't have the least idea where he lives, or what his life is. Now—can we get on with the party? Would you get the mustard down from the top shelf, please?" She was very calm.

"Didn't you want to keep in touch with him?" he said, banging the cupboard door closed. He handed her the jar of mustard.

"Never."

"You liked him once."

"True." She got the chocolate-covered mints from the refrigerator. "Put these in a candy dish, Marcus, and there are some filled mints somewhere."

Marcus poured the mints into the candy dish. "If you liked him once," he persisted, "you could have invited him to see his son sometime. It just seems strange that he never came here, and you never talk about him." He jammed a chair against the wall, finding it hard to keep a sudden flood of emotion out of his voice.

"Look, don't romanticize our relationship. For a time we thought we were in love, but before you were born, we were through. I've never seen him or wanted to see him since."

Marcus polished silver while his mother folded napkins into triangles and arranged them along the edge of the table. "Does that satisfy your curiosity?" she asked.

He shook his head.

"Marcus, a relationship between two people has to have positive feelings to last. People have to really want to be together and take pleasure in each other's company. Like Bill and me. We're—"

"You're not married," he interrupted.

"Exactly. Bill and I aren't married, and we don't live together, but we're as close as any married couple. Bill was here most of the time when you were growing up. He's been a real father to you—not that other man who doesn't deserve to be honored with the name."

Marcus, who was finding it impossible to even listen to his mother any longer, threw down the polishing cloth and handful of spoons and left the room. "Bill's not my real father," he yelled back from the hall.

"What did you say?" Sally called. "Don't go away like that, Marcus. Come back and talk. You started this, now let's finish it."

He came back, avoiding her eyes. She still had the power to call him back and override his feelings and desires with her own. "Okay. Now you listen, Marcus, and stop acting like a stubborn little boy. I expect more from you. I'm going to be honest with you. When I first discovered I was pregnant I was scared. I was young and inexperienced. I hated him because he wanted to run. He wanted absolutely nothing to do with a baby. It was the farthest thing from his mind. But I wanted you more than anything in the world. Everyone said I shouldn't have you, or I should give you up, but once I knew you were there, I knew I would never give you up. And I never did. And it's worked out, hasn't it, Marcus? We've been happy, haven't we?"

He went to the table and poured some punch into a paper cup. He felt nervous and his lips were dry. He didn't want his mother to think he was dissatisfied or unhappy with her, but he still wanted to know about his father. It made him feel frustrated and guilty and ungrateful. He spread his fingers along the edge of the table. Bill said he had the long strong fingers of a potential pianist. But he wouldn't be a musician. Bill was all right. He liked Bill. Of all the men he knew, he liked Bill the best.

He played some imaginary chords along the table as he'd seen Bill do at the piano. He'd do that sometimes when he was sitting down in school, or at home, or on the bus. He'd start playing an imaginary piano, or a bass viol. People would look at him moving his hands back and forth and think, Ah! A musical genius! He ran his fingers rapidly up and down the table. Bong, boing, bong bong! and then a few crashing chords in the bass.

"Marcus?"

He paused, his left hand poised in the air. "Yes?"

84

"Believe me, there are things that are of the past that belong in the past. Your father is one of them."

"I just want to know his name and where he lives. In case somebody asks me someday."

"I thought they didn't ask."

"They don't, but you never know." He was sick of talking about it. She had all the reasons. She didn't have to keep explaining, he understood everything. Why was she making such a fuss about his father's name, though? It was such a little matter—yes, that's what she'd say, but he had to know. The more she refused, the stronger the desire inside him grew. It had nothing to do with sense, or reason, or anything he could readily explain. He just had to know. His mother tried to smooth his hair. He jerked away. "No," he said, "leave me alone." It was what he'd always suspected and feared; it was why he'd gone first to Bill and then to his grandmother. Sally was never going to tell him anything. No matter what he said, or how he argued or pleaded, she would tell him nothing. He'd always known his mother could be single-minded, but it was only now that he felt how strong she really was, like iron, able to say no, and no, and no again.

When the party began, Marcus stood at the door with his mother till Bill came. His mother greeted her friends, kissing and embracing men and women alike. "It's a homecoming party for Bill, when he gets here, the wretch," she laughingly told her guests, "and it's a Thanksgiving party but don't look for the turkey or pumpkin pie. It's also a thank-you party for all the parties we've been invited to and haven't had a chance to repay. So thank you for coming."

Marcus received the kisses of his relatives and his mother's friends almost without wincing. Sally kept him so busy he barely had time to think about their confrontation. When he wasn't taking coats and piling them in the bedrooms, he was serving punch, or bringing more cold cuts, or soda out of the refrigerator.

His grandmother, holding her cigarette away, made him bend down so she could kiss him properly on the cheek, and then she drew him away from the door. "Markey, your cheeks are so rosy, you look good enough to eat."

"Grandma! Do I look that fat? I've been trying to diet. Not much luck, though," he said glumly.

"Nonsense," she squeezed his arm. "You're perfect. Sally," she said, turning to his mother, "are you telling this boy he needs to diet."

His mother, who had been talking to some of her friends from work, came over to kiss her mother. "You look wonderful, Ma. Marcus loves to worry about unimportant things. I tell him not to look back and to concentrate on the future. Isn't that right, Marcus?"

No, it wasn't right! The feeling in his chest was like scalding water. His mother hadn't convinced him of anything. But just then Bill appeared, and she turned to greet him.

"Grandma—" He felt emotion flooding up to his face. "I asked her my father's name, and she won't tell me. Why not, Grandma?"

At the door he saw Sally and Bill kissing, arms

around each other, greeting their friends. She had what she wanted.

His grandmother patted his hand. "Don't get upset, Markey. A party is no time to start asking hard questions."

"But why not, Grandma? Why won't she—"

"I don't know, but your mother has her reasons." She turned to a stout man wearing a bright red vest over green trousers. "Charlie Flowers, I haven't seen you in years. I thought you were dead."

Marcus wandered around the room. People greeted and held him, and then he was wandering again, going over and over the argument with his mother. But what was there to think about? She had said the final word, and that was that. But he couldn't accept it.

"Marcus, my boy." His funny Uncle Albert was making himself a sandwich at the table. He was dressed like a clown with an open baggy jacket and his trousers loose and high over his round belted belly. Uncle Albert, who owned the shoestore, was an amateur magician and for years had played tricks on Marcus, blowing cigar smoke out his ears, or finding a fifty-cent piece in Marcus's nose and then putting it in Marcus's pocket. He called it nose money, or ear money, and it was always for Marcus to keep. His uncle talked and talked. He said so much Marcus sometimes couldn't tell what he was talking about.

"Try the liverwurst on rye, my boy. This is my third one. I recommend it highly, with mustard, and some punch." He took a bite and then wiped the mustard from the corners of his mouth with a hand-kerchief he plucked from his jacket pocket. The handkerchief, once started, seemed to pour out of his pocket in an endless variety of colors, till Uncle Albert snapped his fingers and ordered it to back up. "I keep forgetting you're too old for this sort of child's play. What a pity! But time marches on. Now that you're in junior high and a man, Marcus, what are you going to do with your life? Run for Congress, or run away from home? When I was your age, I had to run away from home. You see, my mother was a certified witch. She had a grocery store and in the back she had cats. Black cats with yellow eyes. She loved those cats more than she did me." He patted his belly. "You may not believe this, Marcus my nephew, but I had to run away from home to save myself. And I never went back. If she caught me she probably would have turned me into a mouse, and fed me to her cats."

"What kind of stories are you telling Marcus?" It was his Aunt Ginny, his mother's sister and Albert's wife, joining them, arm in arm with Sally. "Your mother a witch? Eat your words, Albert. She was a darling woman, Marcus. He only left home because they were terribly poor and needed every penny he earned. Why don't you tell the truth for once, Albert? Why are you always telling fairy stories?"

"Fairy tales contain the wisdom of the ages," Uncle Albert said. "Every young man has to run away from home—the sooner the better."

His mother gave Marcus a conspiratorial smile.

"Marcus is too young and too smart for that, Al. Or were you thinking of running away, darling?"

He felt a dumb anger, a black resentment, a churning of emotion. She didn't know everything about him. She thought she could read his mind, but there were a lot of things she didn't know and would never know. He had plenty of his own private thoughts. And he said grumpily. "I didn't say anything about running away."

His mother's old friend Grace Barrett came late with her daughter in tow. Grace, the teacher, looked like a movie star; she wore velvet pants and high thin heels, and a black velvet ribbon in her slicked-back golden hair. When she kissed him, Marcus flushed with pleasure, her fruit-flavored lipstick remaining like candy on his cheek.

"I brought you Wendy to keep you company," Grace said, standing in the entranceway. Wendy was still in the hall. Like Sally, Grace had only one child, but unlike Sally she'd been married and divorced twice. When Marcus and Wendy were younger they had played together like brother and sister. They had gone on picnics in the mountains and to demonstrations in Washington with their mothers. There was a picture of the two of them in Sally's picture album, when they were little more than babies, standing in a field of daisies, arm in arm, bare except for their panties. They'd remained friends, but as they grew older their contact became more infrequent. Wendy was always a problem to Grace. She was always having trouble handling her. When she was little, Wendy wouldn't eat. And Wendy wouldn't sleep at night. And Wendy didn't cooperate. She talked back to her mother. As she grew older she was often moody and acted in unpredictable ways. She was a problem, a headache, and a burden to Grace.

All this might have gone nearly unnoticed by Marcus if Grace hadn't made a habit of asking Sally how she was able to get along so well with her son. He, Mr. Sane-and-Sober, was encouraged to talk to Wendy, to bring her out when she was moody, to talk sense into her when she was acting like a "nuthatch."

"Talk to her," Grace would tell him. "Find out what's going on in that birdbrain of hers. She looks at me, I think she wants to stick a knife in my heart."

Now Grace stepped into the apartment, but Wendy remained in the hall. "Are you coming in or not?" Grace said. "Or do you expect me to stand here all night holding the door open for you? Come on, coo-coo."

Wendy took exactly one step into the doorway. She wasn't in and she wasn't out.

"Look at her," Grace said, sighing, "did you ever see such a costume?" Wendy was wearing thin, octagonal granny glasses, and her hair was dark, wiry, and standing out all around her head wild as a hawthorn. "She's like from another planet," Grace said. Wendy wore a moldy leopardskin jacket, and a leather thong around her neck with a dried-up piece of root that looked like a shrunken human figure. Dangling from the belt around her ankle-length skirt hung an embroidered pouch, containing, she said, her "powders." And gold hoops through her ears, and bracelets up to her elbow, and rings on every finger. One ring curled like a snake between her knuckles.

"Weird child. Marcus, teach her to be real."

Wendy's face worked as if she were chewing some awful, indigestible thing. Marcus understood exactly how she felt. "Come on," he said, "let's go to my room." And in his room, he said, "I saved you."

"That scene—" Wendy stuck out her tongue. "Blah! I'd like to kill her sometimes. She's such a limited person."

"I don't know why you don't get along with Grace," Marcus said. "Your mother is beautiful, and great fun, too."

"Beautiful on the surface, if that's what you react to. That kind of beauty is skin-deep. Make-up, hair-dos, that movie queen getup, it's a mask. Underneath she's afraid of her own shadow. She's not stupid, either, but all she can think about is men. When she's near a man she's interested in, her brains fall out of her head and she acts like an idiot. And for what? There hasn't been a single man who was worth anything, and that includes my father. Men!" Wendy's lip curled and she gave Marcus her piercing look.

The bed was covered with guests' coats. Wendy had been sitting cross-legged on the floor. Suddenly she slithered like a snake underneath the bed. Bending down he could see her under there, looking out at him. She crooked her finger, motioning him to join her. The dust tickled his nose, and when he turned to make himself comfortable he banged his funny bone.

"Do you always hang out under beds?"

She laughed. "Our own space, you know," she said. "Away from them."

He told her about the fight he'd had earlier with his mother, and how she'd refused to tell him anything about his father. To his astonishment and disgust she defended his mother.

"She's absolutely right, and you're absolutely wrong. Your mother raised you alone. You are completely her son. And, furthermore, you are lucky to have Sally as your mother. Compared to my mother, she's a dream. Why should she let your father have the glory now of showing off for his son when he's never done one thing for you?"

"Boy! I never expected this kind of argument from you," he said. "I thought you'd understand. He is my *father*."

"A biological accident," she said.

"Well, I wouldn't be here without that accident."

"Of course, everyone knows that," she said impatiently. "Marcus, I'm beginning to think you're as dumb as all the other dumb boys I know. So what if you don't know where your father is? I know where mine is, and my stepfather, too, but they might as well not exist for all they do for us. It's our mothers who have done everything for you and me. Brought us up, worked, took care of the house. Well, that should tell you something about what men and women can do. If you want to talk about who's better, is there any question? Our mothers are two truly marvelous women."

"Are you a hypocrite or what?" he demanded. "A minute ago you wanted to kill your mother."

"Mere hyperbole," Wendy said loftily. "I always exaggerate. It makes life more interesting."

He wasn't in the mood to listen to her defend his mother. He'd wanted sympathy.

"Grace thinks I'm weird, but I'm me," she said. "I'm not like anyone else! That's why I dress this way. I don't want to do anything the way my mother does. I don't want to look like her. I won't eat her food. If she forces me, I feed it to my cat when she's not looking. It's vital to maintain your integrity. Do you follow me, Marcus?"

He did and he didn't. He was attracted and re-pelled. What she said sounded a true note—to be his own self, to be somebody. But what if he discovered he was nothing.

"What's the use?" he said. "Our mothers still tell us what to do. We're too young for anything."

"It's not your mother," she said. "You have to want to look beyond the surface of things. It's up to you." She showed him the leather pouch at her waist. She had embroidered it with red stars and a green frog with golden eyes. "It's full of powerful roots and herbs. I'm the frog witch," she said. "I trans-form myself. You can, too. All you have to do is find your true self."

"I don't have your imagination," he said. "I can't."

"Bah!" she said. "I hate the word 'can't.'" She dug her fingernails into the back of his hand. "Believe, Marcus. Believe in the transforming powers of the green frog witch." She sprinkled powders on his hand and on his eyes and over his head. "Now I know why I came here tonight. I hate parties, but I felt you needed me. I heard you crying out for help. Don't laugh, Marcus! I'm here to help you find yourself. Do you want to know who you really are? Do you want to discover your hidden potentialities? Do you know who you are?"

"How's Marcus Rosenbloom?" he said with a grin.

"No! That's the old you. I want you to tell me about the person you're becoming. Tell me about the Marcus to be. How do you see yourself? When you look at your horizon, what do you perceive?"

"I haven't looked at my horizon lately."

"Stop joking," Wendy insisted. "Be serious. You're a hidden city, deep, an unknown country. Learn to resist the easy joke, the easy way. Think, feel deeply! Now, who are you?"

Her words touched something in him. He wanted to answer her. He'd been searching, too, trying to catch a glimpse of himself, sometimes almost coming to something, almost believing, and then it would dissolve, and he was only his old ordinary, overstuffed self. He closed his eyes and concentrated. Who am I? What do I want? He was calling into a darkness that seemed to grow gloomier and more treacherous the louder he called. "I don't know," he cried. "I'm nothing. I'm just a kid. I don't know what I am."

"You can be what you think you are. You can make yourself all the things you hardly dare believe. Marcus, listen to me. Project yourself like a picture on a screen. Enlarge yourself. Blow yourself up big. It's a trick. Then you'll begin to see who you are. A costume helps. Be a witch, be a wizard, be something that will make people's eyes open. The power of the imagination is enough. Now—who are you?"

"Tell me," he said. He felt the power of her insistence, the excitement of a search. He let go of the everyday. He believed. She had the power to tell him what he wanted to know. "Tell me," he said, "what do you see when you look at me?"

"The frog says what matters is what *you* think," she intoned. "What do *you* feel? Tell me about your father. Tell me, Marcus, tell me all the things you feel about him, all the dreams you've had, the things you imagined about your father, but didn't dare say out loud. Speak, Marcus."

"My father is a cowboy—he's an Indian—he's a secret agent—" As he said it, each image seemed to be true. "He's in the mountains on a red horse, searching for rare metals. My father wears boots laced to his knees, he's strong and straight, he's magnificent."

"That's it!" she exclaimed and she hit him with the leather pouch she had in her hand. Dust fell from the bed slats and tickled his nose. "Magnificent! Marcus the Magnificent! *You* are the greatest. You, Marcus the Magnificent," she repeated, and as she said it, he felt it, he believed it. He was that Marcus. He could do anything, be anything, he could make his mother tell him his father's name. Yes, he could!

NINE

MONDAY MORNING Marcus waited for his mother to leave for work. She was telling him to put away the perishables before he left for school and to take out the garbage. He waited, not saying a word. He'd deliberately not spoken to her since the party, in part to punish her, in part to see if he could do it— if he had the power. It was like trying to walk around without opening his eyes. The longer he did it, the harder it was. He hadn't said a word to his mother since the party, only nodding or shaking his head. She'd noticed absolutely nothing, or if she had she'd said nothing. Did it even matter to her what he said? At first he had thought he was really showing her, putting something over on her, but it had gone on now all day Sunday and this morning, and she hadn't even noticed. What was he, a bug, an insect, a speck of nothing?

He felt the flare of renewed anger directed at her. When she left for work he roamed the apartment restlessly, opening and closing doors, kicking obstacles aside. Look out! Suddenly he reached up to the shelf in the hall closet and took down his mother's broad-brimmed black hat and set it squarely on his head. Looking at himself in the mirror, he drew back his lips in a snarl. Then smoothing out his expression, he lifted his eyebrows and with a superior wave of his hand dismissed his bowing, scraping servants. There was a white feather he'd once found on the roof and saved in his bureau drawer. He stuck it into the ribboned brim, cocked the hat to the side of his head, flipped the feather, and lowered his lids over his eyes. He admired himself in the mirror. Marcus the Magnificent. Did he have the nerve to wear the hat to school?

Everybody was sure to say something. Let them! What was it Wendy had told him? He was great. The greatest! She was a witch and knew these things. Yes, he was Marcus the Magnificent. He had only to believe. He did believe. Yes, as long as he wore that hat, he would have magnificent powers.

Look out, here comes Marcus the Magnificent, wearing his Fantastical Hat.

At Bernie's he pushed the McNutley buzzer three times and waited outside. He and Bernie had made up their fight, but there was still an edginess remaining between them because of Marcus's friendship with Dorrity. Bernie acted as if his interest in Dorrity were a betrayal. When Bernie came banging down the steps from the apartment house, Marcus tipped the hat rakishly to one side. "Ah, there you are," he said grandly.

Bernie, his jacket half on, books under one arm, a buttered slice of toast in his mouth, sputtered, "Wha —what the—?" He gestured madly at Marcus, choking down the toast. "Are you wearing that to school?"

97

Marcus cocked the hat even more provocatively to the side. "Why? Why not? What's wrong with you?"

"There's nothing wrong with *me*," Bernie said, stepping away from Marcus, putting distance between them. "You look weird, that's all. What are you trying to do?" he said, turning to look at some kids passing. "Look, everyone's laughing at you. Marcus, you're not going to wear that to school!"

"Yes, I am," Marcus said.

"Who told you to wear that stupid thing? Dorrity? Phillips? Is this one of their wise-ass tricks?"

"You don't know what you're talking about," Marcus said. "You talk about Phillips and Dorrity, but you don't even know them."

"I know enough to know they're a bunch of creeps and snobs. I know all I want to know about them!"

"Ha!" Marcus said, peering out intently from under his hat. "You don't know anything about them, and you've got your mind all made up. Now that's what I call stupid."

"Stupid!" Bernie interrupted. "You're calling *me* stupid! I suppose sucking on the weed is smart!"

"What's wrong with you, McNut? You act like you're still in kindy-garten. Plenty of kids smoke. So what? Just because you don't."

Bernie spit toward the curb. "I'm not just talking about cigarettes, lame-brain. I'm talking about that other stuff. And you know what I mean! I mean that stuff that rots your brains!"

"Are you talking about grass?"

"That's right, lame-brain. All your big, wise friends are on it."

"You're crazy. You don't know what you're talking about."

"I know what I'm talking about, don't you worry!"

"You don't even know Dorrity," Marcus said.

"Who wants to know him? I heard enough about him."

Marcus slapped his side. "Okay, okay, wait a minute, hold it. You said enough. In the first place, everything you've said is opinion and not fact. And in the second place, it's a lie."

"You calling me a liar?" Bernie said, his face tight with anger.

Marcus saw that he'd really stung Bernie. "Look," he said, "I didn't start this argument. You're saying things about my hat and my friends and making a big fuss, and—"

"No fuss, no bother," Bernie said, moving rapidly away from Marcus. "See you, pothead!"

"Hey!" Marcus started after Bernie, sorry they'd quarreled again. Then he stopped and adjusted his hat. He was sick of always making up to Bernie. Instead of following Bernie to their bus stop, he took a turn at the corner toward Dorrity's house.

Dorrity lived on the side of a hill cut off at the bottom by the expressway. A rusty guard rail and a high wire fence blocked the street from the heavy morning traffic. Marcus waited for Dorrity at the head of the street, but the longer he waited the more worried he became. It was getting later and later. He'd already missed his bus, and Dorrity was nowhere in sight. He'd have to run all the way to get to school on time. He crossed to the opposite corner and looked back. He'd count to fifteen. If Dorrity hadn't appeared by then, he'd go. One . . . two . . . three . . . he moved slowly away, looking over his shoulder. At the count of fifteen he broke into a trot.

Soon the back of his ankles began to ache, but he kept trotting and the ache gradually disappeared. The hat kept falling over his eyes, or threatening to fall off his head. And then he saw Dorrity and Phillips and a couple of other kids going by in a battered yellow VW with red fenders. He waved the hat and yelled, "Hey, Dorrity!" but they didn't see him. Rotten luck! And he could have sworn Phillips looked straight at him.

The late bell had rung, and he was hot and sweaty when he got to school. Willis, sitting in the first seat next to the door announced in a loud voice, "You're late, Fat Man."

Marcus swatted at Willis with his hat, and Willis ducked and fell noisily against his desk. "What an entrance you make, Marcus," Mrs. Lord said. "Do you know you're late and need a pass? Where's your pass?"

Marcus nodded and kept going to the back of the room where he dropped down in a seat. He was sweating and the hat was half off his head, the feather tickling his face. He was brooding over Dorrity's not stopping for him. He was sure Dorrity hadn't seen him. If he had, things would have gone differently. Dorrity would have jammed on the brakes of the yellow VW and stopped for him.

Cool Magnificent Marcus, he would have said, *this*

vehicle is at your service. Push over, Phillips. Make room for Marcus!

They would have arrived at school in plenty of time, and stood out in front rapping in the sunshine. Marcus, the center of attention, would be wearing wide flaring trousers with a plate-sized silver buckle, a salt and pepper vest, and his magnificent black cavalier hat with the sweeping white plume.

Vivian would arrive and adjust the plume and arrange the feather so it curled around the brim of the hat. Vivian and Dorrity, his two good friends. Both of them admired his hat. They responded to its beauty and appropriateness. A cool, magnificent hat, fit for a king. King Kool, that was the way he signed his papers. King Kool, or sometimes, Marcus Kool. Always in control in all situations.

Marcus Kool, humble Mrs. Lord said, *what can we expect from you today?*

My magnificent presence, Marcus Kool replied. *I was unfortunately detained on my way to class when my services were required by Mr. Firstman, the vice principal in charge of student coordination.*

Marcus Kool then explained how the vice principal, known to certain fearful students as "The Hitter," had been locked in his office with a half-crazed student. He, Marcus Kool, had coolly and quickly calmed the distraught student without so much as raising his voice. It only took a cool glance, and the student returned to reality. Mr. Firstman's gratitude was boundless. He proposed that Marcus take charge of his office for several hours daily . . .

"Marcus!" Mrs. Lord was speaking to him. "Marcus, how many times do I have to repeat your name and tell you to get up and go to the office for a late pass!"

King Kool slowly rose to his full magnificence. He exited regally, smiting this and that boy on the head with his royal hat.

"The principal wants to discuss school policy. A rap session—"

"Rap you, Marcus," Willis yelled.

"I will return," Marcus said, replacing his feathered hat. It brushed the top of the doorway, tipping backward on his head.

In the office, Mrs. Paoletti was fascinated by Marcus's explanation of his lateness "I missed the bus by less than one second but I was determined to get to school on time."

She twirled the silver peace symbol hanging from her necklace. "Yes—and then what happened?"

Did she realize he'd nearly lost his life in a heroic effort to catch the bus? He'd reached it just as the door was closing. He'd barely gotten his fingers in the door when it slammed shut and the bus moved away, the driver unaware of Marcus's presence. He'd run with the bus at top speed for three blocks before he'd managed to free his fingers. It was fortunate that he was in such superb physical condition and was able to sprint alongside a rapidly moving bus.

"After that, I ran twenty blocks to school," Marcus said. "I was entering the door when the late bell rang."

"It's a wonder your nose doesn't grow long and get pinched in the door, the stories you tell." She

pushed the late pass across the counter. "Too many
of these, and it's Mr. Firstman for you. And I don't
think he's very partial to the story hour."

Marcus clutched his stomach in mock fear of Mr.
Firstman, the notorious Hitter. And King Kool added
his thanks. "You're an extremely gracious lady."

In the halls, passing to classes, Marcus the Magnificent kept his hat proudly in place. The more people
pointed to him, the taller he stood. When Willis's
voice rang out, "Hey, King Lard," he responded,
"King Kool to you, termite." But going into the biology lab he nearly tripped over Mr. Lange's desk. For-
tunately, Mr. Lange was not there. Recovering, Marcus
bowed to the skeleton that had just been wheeled in
by the audio-visual boys and placed in front of the
window. "How do you do?" he said, and impulsively
placed his plumed hat over the skeleton's naked head.

"Who's the new student, Rosey? Your skinny sister?"

Karen Sweet ran up front and stuck a yellow pencil
between the skeleton's jaws.

"This is Greta, a Princess of the Royal House,"
Marcus said.

A pair of mismatched sneakers came flying up front
for Greta's feet, and a scarf was produced for her
neck.

"Is it really a woman's skeleton," Pete Fuller yelled.
"How can you tell? She's awfully flat-chested."

"Yuk yuk," someone responded.

"It has one less rib."

"It's smaller."

"If it's a her, she's missing an important part, ha,
ha, ha!"

"It's Marcus's sister. What's the matter, don't you feed her?"

Marcus, who had been standing by Greta with a proprietary air, found himself defending her. "Not my sister, but *somebody*, you nits!" Whoever the skeleton was, he was sure it wasn't a teacher, or a principal of a school. People like that didn't get boiled down to their bare bones and strung up like a clothes tree. "It's probably some poor person who couldn't defend herself. Who gets cut up and pulled apart, poked and practiced on by a lot of clumsy medical students, and then has her parts put in jars for everyone to look at forever? Not the rich, the influential, or the famous!"

"Right on, judge!"

Warming to the role of Skeleton's Advocate, Marcus the Magnificent strode to the front of the court and pointed a finger at the jury. "No, ladies and gentlemen of the jury," he said dramatically, "no member of the acting profession, or the Congress of the United States, no rich man or industrial giant ever found himself, after death, pickled in a jar. And, I might add respectfully, no member of this jury will, either." He paused, a finger in the air, aware of the strong impression he was making on the jury. "Only the poor," he said, dropping his voice. "The poor, the weak, the defenseless."

The class was going wild. "Right on, Perry Mason!" Pete Fuller and Carl Simon were chasing each other around the room. A storm of paper balls hit Greta. There were cheers and catcalls.

"Marcus, are you from the National Association for the Protection of Skeletons?" Karen Sweet called.

"The National Association is a noble organization—" Marcus began, but Mr. Lange's appearance cut him off and sent everyone racing for his seat. Only Marcus was still at the window.

Mr. Lange pointed a neatly manicured finger at the class. "Take your place, Rosenbloom. My place is here, your place is there."

"That's my hat. Can I get it?"

Mr. Lange gazed at skinny Greta, then slowly shook his head. "Leave it right where it is and take your seat."

"But it's mine," Marcus said.

"Do I have to repeat myself, Rosenbloom?" Their eyes met. Marcus was a head taller than Mr. Lange, but when Mr. Lange told him to sit down and shut up, he sat down and shut up. Without his hat, gloom descended on Marcus. He hated the way he agreed with grownups even when he disagreed with them. He was that way with Bill, he was that way with his mother, and now he'd done it again. When Mr. Lange removed the hat from Greta and dropped it into a desk drawer and told Marcus he could retrieve it in the office after school, he didn't say a word. What could he say? What could he do? The hat in Mr. Lange's drawer might as well be a million miles away. If he really had the powers Wendy had conferred on him, he wouldn't have asked Mr. Lange anything. He would have snatched the hat from Greta's bony dome and popped it onto his own head. If Mr. Lange had objected he would have told *him* to sit down and shut up! But he didn't have the nerve, because that Magnificent Marcus, that King Kool, that master of all situations wasn't really him.

He sat in back of the room, hating the class, the school, and himself. All he could do was dream that his father had come to school with him and told everyone off. *My son Marcus wants his magnificent hat back. Now!* When his father spoke, people listened. Marcus sat there, smiling to himself, thinking how his father would make Mr. Lange scurry to give his son Marcus back his hat.

His mother wanted to talk to Marcus. "Why am I getting calls from school? They never called from Prescott. You were a good student. Now, in Columbus, all I hear is complaints. Why?"

She was seated on the plaid chair near the dining room table, the potted green rubber plant behind her. Bill was at the table, reading some music.

"They say you've been late several times. They say you've been acting up. Are you having trouble getting up in the morning? I'll be glad to help you."

"It only happened once."

"And there was something about showing off, making a display of yourself wearing a big black hat. What was that all about? Is something wrong, Marcus? I never thought of you as a show-off before."

"I'm not a show-off." He kicked the black and white hassock across the room. The teachers were a bunch of squint-eyed, jealous, narrow-minded creeps. They were afraid of anyone stepping out of line, showing their individuality. There was no justice, or respect for the individual. "If you act yourself, they all jump on you."

"You're talking foolishly," his mother said. "Now, settle down, Marcus, this is Sally and Bill you're talking to. We all understand each other. Not being on time, acting up in school, what does that have to do with justice and individual rights? Your teachers have a right to respect. Rules have to be followed."

What about him, didn't he deserve respect, too? Everyone was so quick to tell him what he was doing wrong. What about the wrong they did? Marcus was filled with an overwhelming sense of injustice; his eyes stung. The grownup world was far, far from perfect. He hadn't done anything except wear a hat to school and skip out on study hall. That didn't exactly make him the biggest criminal in the United States.

"Why are you getting so upset?" his mother said. "What's happened? You were never like this before." She talked about showing good sense, of not disappointing her, of being the sensible, thoughtful boy she knew he was. She talked and talked, and he could feel the resentment and stiffness grow in himself, almost gagging him. She wasn't treating him like a person either, no matter what she said. Why didn't she tell him the truth and let him judge for himself?

"The truth," he choked.

"What?" She looked up, startled. "What are you talking about?"

"My father," he said.

He saw her stiffen. "The truth," she said, "is one thing you can be sure you've always gotten from me. I never lied to you. I've been straight with you. I don't regret anything. I brought you up. I love you. I was mother and father both. And there's nothing wrong with the way you are."

"Bravo," Bill said.

His mother started to laugh. "Well, I guess I made a speech, didn't I, Marcus? Go wash your face, you're all flushed. There's some cake and milk for you in the refrigerator," she added, as calmly as if nothing had happened.

He started to go, then he came back.

"What is it, Marcus?"

"Nothing," he said. "Nothing!" There were too many things going on inside him, too many racing, conflicting feelings and ideas. He couldn't get them all into words. He didn't know where to start. What was the matter with him? Why wasn't he a better person? Sometimes he thought he was crazy, the things he felt like doing. Like loving his mother one minute and wanting to hold her mouth shut the next.

Later, lying on his bed, he looked out the window, out across the courtyard to the lighted windows in the opposite building. He saw a man standing on a chair and changing a light bulb in the ceiling. In another window a woman in a yellow slip was vacuuming the floor. Another window was empty except for a rose-colored wall showing between half-drawn drapes. There were so many things to see out there.

There were so many rooms he wanted to see into, so much to learn, so much to experience. He felt he would burst if he had to stay there forever, and then he felt that his back was growing into the bedding under him, growing and spreading soft and shapelessly, like a fat white slug.

His mother wouldn't understand that, but his father . . . if only he knew his father. If he could see him and talk to him, without having to make up the stories he was always telling himself. Once he'd showed Bernie a picture that his mother had on the living room wall, a painting of a young man with full red lips. It was a painting by a famous artist, but he'd told Bernie that this was his older brother Vincent who was with his father collecting snakes and monkeys and other wild animals in the Amazon jungle for zoos and scientists all over the world. And for a while he had Bernie almost believing it.

Stories, fairy tales, lies! Marcus hated the stories he told. What were they, but just a way of making believe he had something he didn't. It made him feel bigger than he was. Marcus Kool. King Kool. That was a joke. King Lard was what he was. Willis was right. King Lard. King Shit.

He hated himself and his life so thoroughly in that moment that he was ready at a word to spring out of the window and tell himself to fly. Just like his stories. If he fell that would solve everything, and if his stories were real, he'd fly straight to his father, no matter where.

He imagined himself rising up from the bed and

floating out the window, just clearing the terrace railing, out across the empty courtyard, up over the roofs, and chimneys, and TV antennas. The feeling was so strong he almost believed it was happening, but when he looked around he was still lying on his bed, looking out the window up into the blank sky.

TEN

MORE AND MORE Marcus stayed away from home. He felt at odds with his mother. They weren't arguing. The arguments were all in his head. He simply avoided being where she was. He ate early and went out, leaving notes on the table: "I ate, be back later . . . At Bernie's . . . Working late for Rossi . . ."

When he came in he went quickly to the bathroom and then to his room. When his mother tried to question him he said he was tired. They could talk in the morning. But in the morning he said he had homework he'd forgotten. But he wasn't doing his schoolwork. He was going along on luck and hoping he could bluff when he had to answer questions. And he wasn't seeing Bernie.

He spent all the time he could with Dorrity, hanging out near the Shopping Plaza, the laundromat in bad weather and the doughnut shop when they were hungry. That was where he found the group one afternoon. It was nearly dusk. Phillips balanced on a fire hydrant, one hand on Bisner's head. Jeff Wine, Phillips's cousin, was with them. "Rosenbloom," Dorrity said, "how much money have you got?"

Marcus produced a crumpled dollar. "You're in!"

Phillips hopped down from the hydrant, snatched the dollar, and handed it to Dorrity, who went into the Big Market where he sometimes worked bagging. He emerged with three six-packs of beer in a paper bag. "Let's go." He led the way down the street toward the parkway and they all followed.

Across the double lane of expressway traffic they ran to the swatch of green grass, and then, waiting for a break, across the other double lane of traffic. On the top of a low concrete building a new billboard was being erected. A huge fringed blue eye met Marcus's eyes. Under it the words FAIR PLAY LOANS. If you believed in mystical signs, everything had meaning. A break in the fence, cracks in the sidewalk, three pigeons soaring in the air. There were signs everywhere. The blue eye followed Marcus. It said, Pay Attention. It said, Fair Play. Fair play: that was exactly what he wanted from his mother.

Dorrity led the way into empty fenced lots where the old buildings had been torn down and the new ones not yet begun. The empty lots were like fields, the weeds grown up wild and uneven. Above them was the cool open sky. The fields, the yellow grass, the space and freedom went to their heads. Almost as one they started running, Dorrity in front, the others following in a long ragged line. Running and running across widening fields to where pale silvery metal sheds stood, and stacks of concrete pipe, and wooden forms, and steel beams and yellow earth-moving machines—bulldozers, cranes, and scrapers crowded together like prairie animals in the dusk.

Against a fragment of brick wall that had somehow remained standing, they built a fire from dry paper stuck in the stiff grass and scraps of wood. A good wind was blowing. The boys sprawled by the fire, separated from the parkway by the great space of the cleared land. Alone, cut off from the city, half hidden in the empty lot, on their own. Except for the roar of the expressway, they could have been Indians on a western plain, Marcus thought, or Mongol horsemen on the Asian steppes, or buffalo hunters settling down for the night.

Dorrity tore open the paper bag and set down the beer packs. Beer cans were passed around, hissing as the aluminum keys were pried out, and the cans raised. Marcus raised his with the others. He lounged and sprawled out, his feet toward the fire, elbows over a charred telephone pole at his back. The wind died away and then returned, the smoke curled and turned and blew in their faces. Marcus tipped up his can, long and steady, letting the clear, cold yellow liquid, with its maltish, almost unpleasant, aftertaste, spill down his gullet. He leaned back, enjoying the closeness of his companions. Phillips breath boiled in his ear. Jeff Wine, the cousin, a short handsome boy with big eyes, had his sneakered legs over Marcus's knee.

"Who's got his foot up my back end?" Jeff said lazily.

"Quiet, or you die," Bisner said. "Watch this." He spit into the air. The spittle arced up, bright in the darkness, and then fell sizzling into the fire. The others tried, sometimes falling short, sometimes hitting the target. Bisner claimed to be the champion spitter, but Phillips had a cool, neat way of hitting the fire every time.

Bisner lit a cigarette and passed it to Dorrity, who took a deep drag and passed it on to Marcus. Marcus hesitated, thinking it might be marijuana, then put the cigarette to his lips. It was just a regular cigarette. He held it the way Dorrity had, the lighted end turned in toward his palm, puffing on it, the cigarette hidden in his hand.

"Don't waste it on him," Bisner said, snatching it away. "Look what he did to the tip—he spit on it." He showed Dorrity the wet tip. "He spit on it!" he howled.

"What are you talking about?" Dorrity said. "You wet it yourself, leaky mouth. Leave the kid alone."

"He spit on it, I tell you."

"Shut up," Dorrity said. Then he ordered Bisner to put up his fists. "I'm going to demonstrate a little championship sparring." Bisner reluctantly put up his hands. "See how it's done," Dorrity said, flicking Bisner in the nose. "See that lightning left jab. That's how you keep him off balance." In the light of the fire, Dorrity was like a young lion, sandy hair falling smoothly over his forehead, his freckled, square-knuckled hands poised in the air.

The beer went around again. Marcus received his share, more than he'd ever drunk at one time before. He felt really at ease. This was real friendship, the comradeship of older boys, the brotherhood of young men. The future, the past, all the things that had bothered him—all of that seemed unimportant now.

What he wanted and what his mother wanted, the dissatisfied feelings, and the things that had seemed so difficult to him before, now faded away like the last light into the night. He leaned back, shaking his head slowly from side to side. He was a little dizzy. The beer had gone to his head.

Jeff Wine was talking about a girl he and Phillips knew. "She's crazy about guys. We should have brought her, right, cousin?"

"What's that?" Marcus said, waking from his dream of contentment. "What did you say?"

"I said," Jeff said, "if this girl I know was here, she'd grab you right there." And he leaned toward Marcus and grabbed at his thigh.

Marcus reacted. "Cut it out!"

"What are you so jumpy about?" Jeff said, making as if to grab Marcus again. "Look at him jump," Wine said happily to the others. "Watch this. He jumps like a frog. He's goosy as a girl." He grabbed at Marcus's crotch and Marcus reacted as he had before, jumping back, exclaiming, "Cut it out!" and then grabbed Jeff around the waist. The two of them rolled on the ground, with the others springing aside and yelling encouragement. Rolling and trying to pin each other down, squirming free and grabbing, arm lock and scissors lock, till Marcus, heavier and bold with beer, sat triumphantly on Jeff's chest, hot and laughing up at Dorrity, who saluted him and handed him another can of beer.

Marcus drank and Jeff protested. "Get your big ass off me."

Marcus poured the beer over Jeff's head and fell to

one side, laughing and drunk and filled with wonderful feelings of power and contentment.

The last beers were passed around. It was late. The empty bag, cardboard, everything that would burn was thrown on the fire, which blazed higher. The wind sprang up, blowing sheets of crackling plastic across the empty fields. Dorrity had his hands in his pocket. "Time to call out the fire department," Phillips said. Dorrity nodded, and they all unzipped their flies and peed on the fire. The fire smoldered, the smoke rising thick, acrid, and stinking of urine.

As they crossed the black fields they sang "Here comes the sun, here comes the sun," arms around each other's shoulders. Then they sang "Irene" and "Twenty more miles to go." As they came out on the expressway, a green and white police car swung around and came toward them.

"Run," Dorrity said, and the five of them dived under the fence, propelled like Peter Rabbit out of Mr. McGregor's garden, running alongside the fence till they came to Almond Street and safety, and stood there laughing and hot before they went their separate ways home.

Marcus was out of breath, he had a stitch in his side, and his ankles hurt from running, but he felt wonderful and powerful. He wasn't drunk, maybe a little high. Not exactly floating. His feet were on the ground, but very, very light. He started home, talking to his mother. No, *telling* his mother. No more talking! No more discussions! He wanted to know about his father. Everything! Name! Address! Phone number! Nothing held back. And he wasn't babying his

mother's feelings either. He was going to see his
father, and that was that. He was no longer Momma's
little boy.

Going home he was aware of how tall he stood, so
light on his feet he barely touched the ground. People
smiled at him as he passed. "*Hi* there," he raised his
arm in greeting. He felt very friendly, very good
about himself, filled with those easy, in-the-world,
Marcus-the-Magnificent feelings. Just fine!

In the elevator of his building three little girls were
standing near the door, two in jeans and one wearing
Bugs Bunny flannel pajamas and fluffy pink slippers.
Behind them was an old man wearing a sporty plaid
hat. A glance and Marcus's computer-like mind regis-
tered every detail.

"*Hi* there, how are you all this evening?" He smiled
broadly, his voice taking on the slurred intonation of
a popular singer, an effect he thought very mature
and appropriate. He felt relaxed with this old man,
looking him in the eyes. "These elevators sure are
slow, man."

The man looked at him, his face expressionless,
only his mouth working in and out like a pulse.

"You know how to make the elevator go faster?"
Marcus said to the three little girls. He bent his
knees, then straightened up, "Go-ooo, elevator!"

The doors shut and the elevator started smoothly
up. "See what I mean," Marcus said. He stood smiling
at the doors till his floor was reached. The doors
opened, and still he stood there.

"This your floor?" the man behind him said.

"This is my floor, my floor, the floor I own," Marcus

sang, stepping out. The hall was like a tunnel, dim
and yellow and filled with loud music and a smell of
onions, grease, and meat that seemed to curl around
Marcus's stomach.

In the apartment Sally was sitting on the arm of
Bill's chair. Bill had his shoes off. His mother's hair
was untied. She had her arm around Bill's shoulder.
The stereo was playing, and on the stove the kettle
boiled.

"*Hi* there," Marcus said.

"Hi there yourself," Bill said. "I was afraid I
wouldn't see you. This is my last night in the city.
Tomorrow I'm off on a Canadian tour."

"Marcus?" Sally stood up and smelled his breath.
"Have you been drinking? He's been drinking, Bill.
He smells like a brewery!"

Bill laughed. "Phew! some brew."

The tea kettle in the kitchen whistled piercingly.
"What's the idea, Marcus?" his mother said. "Since
when have you been drinking?"

"The hot water, Sally," Bill said. "The tea kettle
calls." He winked at Marcus.

Sally went to the kitchen, saying, "It's those new
friends of yours, isn't it?"

Bill sat back. "You're turning into a boozer at an
early age, Marcus."

"I'm not drunk," Marcus said with as much dignity
as he could muster. "I know exactly what I'm doing."
He didn't feel drunk. He felt sick. His stomach was
gurgling unpleasantly.

His mother appeared with a tray of cups, saucers,

and cookies. "Come on, you two, give a hand here. The maid is out for the season."

"Marcus, old man, give me a hand." Bill put out his hand and Marcus pulled energetically, almost pulling the two of them over. Bill put his arm around Marcus's shoulder. "Easy, partner, that was some pull."

"Come over here, Marcus, and sit down. You need a cup of tea to settle your stomach." His mother put her hand on his forehead. "Do you have a fever? How's your stomach?"

He pushed her hand away. "Don't hover over me," he said. "I want to talk seriously." He thumped his hand on the table, rattling the dishes. "Right now!"

"And I want to talk to *you* seriously," his mother said. "I don't like drinking. You don't have to drink, and you don't have to run around with a gang to be a real man. Bill will back me up. This male machismo baloney! Nobody has to drink. There's too much drinking and fighting in the world. If you have to prove how big you are, do it some constructive way. Be an athlete, or a scientist. Be a musician."

"The serious thing I want to talk to you about," Marcus said carefully, trying to ignore the sick feeling that was rising in his throat, "is I believe I'd like to visit my father. A visitation," he added grandly. It was funny the way it came out. "So if you'll please give me his name and address, Sally, and his phone number, I'll be obliged."

His mother's hands went up in the air. "That again. It's impossible. You must really be drunk to be talking this way."

"I am not drunk," he said, enunciating each word with precision. "Why is it impossible?" and spluttering in his excitement, he added, "Why? Why, why, why? Other kids see their fathers even when they don't live together. Why can't I?"

"We've talked about it enough," his mother said. "I don't want to talk about it anymore. Certainly not on Bill's last night."

"You say you treat me like a real person, but you don't. You don't treat me like an equal. You tell me what you'll talk about, and what you won't. Real people have to learn for themselves, but you won't let me learn anything for myself. And that's dis-honest! *Dis*-honest!"

"You're drunk," she said.

"Maybe I'm drunk, but it's the truth."

Bill, quiet till now, said, "Listen to him, Sally. He's only saying what you yourself believe. And what you've brought him up to believe."

Sally made a fist. "Shut up, Bill! You're no help at all. You're as good as calling me a hypocrite."

"I didn't say that. I only said Marcus has an argu-ment when he says he's old enough to make up his own mind."

Sally started to reply, then put her hands to her mouth and leaned forward in her chair. After a mo-ment she said, "All right. You talk, Marcus. Say what you've got to say. I've said too much already."

Marcus sat there, feeling miserable. His stomach was churning. "Tell me his name," he said finally.

"I can't say the man's name," Sally said emotionally. "I swore I'd never say his name again."

"Write it down, Sally," Bill said, producing a pencil and a scrap of paper from a pocket.

"You don't give a woman a chance, do you?" she said and ran from the room, only to return immediately. "I don't know—this has gone on long enough. Maybe you two are right. I can't tell anymore." And while Marcus watched in a daze of nausea and triumph, she hastily scrawled his father's name and where he had lived fourteen years ago.

ELEVEN

IT WAS EARLY in the morning. Marcus rushed through the streets, alive with the news of his father's name. George Renfrew. He laughed; he had guessed so many names. George Renfrew—it sounded just right. Years ago he'd thought his father's name was just like his own—Rosenbloom. Dumb! Really dumb! That was his mother's name. Even knowing his grandmother's name was Rosenbloom, and his Uncle Stan was Rosenbloom, and his Aunt Ginny had been Rosenbloom—how could his father be Rosenbloom? His father's name had to be something else.

George Renfrew, it sounded good to Marcus, the ease with which he said it. George Renfrew and his son Marcus. Maybe, someday, he'd change his name. Marcus Renfrew. Boys carried their father's names. Girls, too, for that matter.

Marcus ran into a doorway and studied the names under the mailboxes, and on the bell boards. He ran into another doorway and another. His father could be anywhere—on this block, around the corner. A thousand people lived on every block and there had to be a thousand blocks in the city, maybe ten thousand . . .

He stepped into a phone booth and looked up the name Renfrew in the directory. There were a dozen Renfrews, but only one Renfrew on the North Side where his father had lived. Neal Renfrew. His father's brother? Then the man would be his uncle. His mother had said something, too, about the Renfrew family having once owned a variety store on Canal Street. "But that's all I'm going to say," she'd added. "I don't want you hurt. I suppose that's overly protective, but I can't help it. You and Bill have talked me around—now you'll have to find out for yourself."

Marcus dialed Neal Renfrew's number. It was early, but people were up for work. The phone kept ringing. What if his father was visiting his brother and answered the phone. What would he say to him? *Hello, this is Marcus Rosenbloom, your son . . .*

He was so excited he could barely stand there with the phone to his ear. And it was still ringing. Nobody was going to answer. He hung up reluctantly. Then a new idea seized him. Dorrity used to live on the North Side. He was always talking about how much better things used to be there. It was so weird. Dorrity on the North Side, and his father on the North Side. It had to mean something. What if Dorrity knew Neal Renfrew? Or George Renfrew? Or any Renfrews?

Before, when he hadn't even known his father's name, he'd put his father anywhere and everywhere —north, east, south, west. On every continent and in every ocean. He'd even imagined his father on one of the space voyages. But now that he knew his father had lived there in the city, worked there, known his mother there—it was far better, infinitely more exciting. But if his father's name wasn't in the phone book, did it mean he had moved? And how would he find him?

Dorrity would have ideas. He hurried to school eager to see Dorrity, but he didn't find him at once. He wasn't in the crowded corridor by the front stairs, or in his homeroom, or in Mr. Miller's room where they sometimes went to talk. Finally he found Dorrity and Phillips at the bottom of the stairwell in back of the gym. Marcus entered the stairwell noisily and they both looked up at him. The light was dim and he couldn't see them plainly. "Dorrity," he called, clattering down the stairs.

"It's okay," Phillips said, "it's only young Rosenbloom." His strong teeth glistened in a sardonic grin.

Dorrity had a cigarette hidden in his hand, and in case a teacher came Phillips had the outside door partially open for a fast exit. Marcus had noticed the smell the minute he entered the stairwell, not the smell of an ordinary cigarette. But he didn't think about it. "I've got his name," he shouted exuberantly.

Dorrity gave him that unquenchable smile. "What do you say, kid? Whose name?"

"George Renfrew, my father's name. He used to live where you used to live, on the North Side, near the Iron Works. Maybe you knew him. George Renfrew."

"Great," Dorrity said, glancing at the slip of paper on which Sally had scribbled his father's name and street.

"Raymond Street, you used to live there, didn't you?"

"Near there, on Milton Avenue." Dorrity handed the butt to Phillips and looked at the paper more carefully. Marcus looked over Dorrity's shoulder, spelling his father's name for him. He wasn't aware of Mr. Firstman, the vice principal, standing at the head of the stairs, peering down at them.

Phillips, next to the door, saw Mr. Firstman and hissed a warning to Dorrity.

"Jesus!" Dorrity dropped Marcus's paper and sprang after Phillips, who was already out the door.

"Stand where you are," The Hitter shouted. "None of you boys move." The man's voice resounded down the stairs.

Marcus would have run, too, but he had to retrieve the paper with his father's name. When he bent to grab it the stream of air from the closing door blew it just out of his reach so that he had to scramble for it on his knees. And then the vice principal was on top of him.

"Okay, you, on your feet." He grabbed Marcus's arm and pulled him up, then pushed him against the wall. "Stand still and don't move." He bent over to pick up the smoldering butt from the floor where Phillips had thrown it. He pinched off the ash and sniffed it. "Marijuana," he said triumphantly. "I smelled it all the way up the stairs. I know you. I know those others, too. You stand right there."

He ran out the door after Phillips and Dorrity. Marcus turned and started up the stairs. Smoking in school was a minor offense. The teachers did it all the time. But marijuana—Dorrity and Phillips were really stupid! He knew it was grass; he had smelled it, too.

But still it had nothing to do with him. He hadn't been smoking.

He was just turning into his homeroom when The Hitter came flying after him, collared him, and before the startled eyes of his class, ordered him to the office. He propelled Marcus down the stairs, demanding in a loud voice, "Who were they, Rosenbloom? Who were the others?" In the outer office, he shoved Marcus down on the long wooden bench. "Just sit there till I get back. Don't move. That's an order! Mrs. Paoletti, this boy isn't to move from this office!" Then he was gone again.

Marcus sat alone, his back against the glass wall. If he turned he could see out into the hall where the kids were passing to classes, but mostly he sat with his elbows on his thighs, looking at his shoes. He sat there a long time. Kids coming in and out of the office glanced at him sympathetically, but he didn't invite them to ask questions. He felt very strange. Separated. He had done nothing, he didn't belong here, but here he was, on the spot. Worst of all, he couldn't help feeling guilty.

Mr. Firstman walked by him. "Don't move." Then he disappeared into his office.

Marcus wished Dorrity and Phillips were here. They'd explain everything. *Look, the kid is clean,* Dorrity would say. *He was just standing there, talking to me. He wasn't smoking.*

Mrs. Paoletti shook her head. "You blew it this time. I'm sure your mother is going to be very proud of you."

"I was just standing by the stairs and The Hitter grabbed me."

"Mr. Firstman is the name. You kids are so smart about some things, but you can be really dumb about other things. If you don't think getting caught smoking marijuana in school isn't serious, you need to have your brains unscrambled."

"I wasn't smoking—" But the skeptical look she gave him made him stop. In Mrs. Paoletti's eyes he was caught, convicted, and ready for jail.

"If Mr. Firstman caught you, you're in serious trouble. He's been trying to get one of you kids on the weed all year. You're the first one. You're the example. He's going to throw the book at you." She nodded toward the principal's office. "He's in there right now, trying to reach your home."

Marcus didn't reply. He folded his arms over the hard lump of his stomach pressing against his belt, and pushed back hard against the bad feelings. He wished Mr. Firstman would come out now and get this thing over with. Every time the principal's door opened, his stomach turned over.

He sat in the office for the entire morning, watching the clock, watching every person who came and went. It was fifth period and classes were changing when he saw Bernie peering through the glass. Marcus got up.

"You cannot leave this office," Mrs. Paoletti said.

Marcus gestured to Bernie to come in. He was glad to see his friend. He needed somebody who believed him. "It's all over school, Marc. Everybody's talking about you being busted."

"I didn't do anything. I was just standing there."

"Who was it?" Bernie interrupted. "Was it Dorrity?"

Marcus glanced over his shoulder, afraid Mrs. Paoletti was listening. "You better not hang around here," he said. After Bernie left, Marcus felt worse than ever. His lunch period came and went and still nothing had happened. Mr. Firstman was in and out of the office, half the time acting as if he didn't see Marcus. Shortly after the last bell, he finally motioned Marcus into his office.

"Shut the door," he said. "Sit down." His office was small. If Marcus stretched out his arms he could touch both walls. He felt trapped. The Hitter had a reputation for always getting what he wanted from a student. "Okay, Rosenbloom." He stood behind his desk, tapping a pencil in his hand. "I want your story. Tell me exactly what happened. When I saw you, you were trying to hide something under the stairs. A lighted roach." He tapped a small brown envelope with the pencil, a significant smile on his face. "I've got the evidence right here."

Marcus cleared his throat. "I wasn't smoking."

"I saw you myself."

"I was looking for a piece of paper that fell down."

"And the lighted roach?"

"I don't know anything about it."

"It was just lying there, smoking itself. Beautiful." Mr. Firstman's voice dripped sarcasm, and then abruptly he raised his voice, lashing out. "You want me to believe that! You think anyone is that stupid to believe you were kneeling, unaware, next to a lighted marijuana cigarette. Because that's what it smelled

128

like, and that's what it looked like, and that's what the lab is going to tell us it is when we take you before the Superintendent of Schools and he expels you. It was marijuana, wasn't it?"

"No, sir." Then Marcus corrected himself. "I don't know."

"You don't know?"

"Someone else was smoking."

"Ahh, someone else, of course. And who was that?"

Marcus shook his head. Why had he said anything? Where was Dorrity now when he needed him?

"You don't know, you're shaking your head, you don't know anything. Of course you know. You want me and the principal and the Superintendent of Schools to believe you were crawling around under the stairs looking for a slip of paper and didn't know the someone who was smoking almost next to you. Don't forget, I saw them, too."

Marcus, clinging to the only truth he could repeat, said, "I wasn't smoking. I didn't smoke anything."

"Oh, yes, you did! It doesn't make any difference if you were the one smoking at that moment or not. You were holding that roach. Possession is as damaging as smoking."

"I wasn't—" Marcus said.

"And you were passing it back and forth. It's just too bad the other ones got away. But we've got you. You're in serious trouble, Rosenbloom, and it's going to get a lot worse if you don't tell me their names. You not only broke the school rules, you broke the law of this state as well."

Marcus was sweating. He couldn't think. He felt

frightened and angry. Why didn't the man believe him? He hadn't done anything.

There was a long silence. At last Mr. Firstman sat down, folded his hands, and smiled at Marcus. "I understand, Marcus," he said, nodding. "The others are guiltier than you. They're older, for one thing. We're not completely blind to what's been going on. I've almost caught them several times." There was another long pause. "You believe that people who break rules should be punished?" Marcus nodded mutely. "Of course you do. You don't defend drugs, I'm sure, or the guilty. Are you guilty?"

"No!" It felt good to break his sweating silence, to say the simple truth. "No, Mr. Firstman."

"Of course you're not," the vice principal said soothingly. "It's the others, isn't it? Who are they, Marcus?" he said in a gentle voice.

Marcus was silent. He felt sweat under his armpits. He became aware of his hands gripping the edge of the chair. He loosened them, feeling that Mr. Firstman, whose eyes never left his, saw everything. He made himself return the man's looks. He wasn't lying. He had to stick to the simple truth till Dorrity came forward, as Marcus knew he would, to tell the whole story for himself. It didn't matter what Mr. Firstman said. He, Marcus, couldn't say Dorrity's name first, couldn't be the one to get Dorrity, his friend, into trouble.

"James Dorrity. Don Phillips. Weren't those the two boys that slipped away?"

Marcus's heart jumped. He blinked rapidly, biting

at his lips. He tried to make his face a blank, sure he'd given it away.

Mr. Firstman banged his hands on the desk. "You're defying me!" Marcus wanted to look away, but kept his face turned toward the man. "On your feet!" Mr. Firstman ordered. "I ought to shut your lying mouth. What do you mean, lying to me? You were with two other boys, and you know who they were."

Marcus's mouth was dry. Something inside him was flickering and exploding, quieting, and exploding again. He stood there and waited, the palms of his hands wet, his face swollen. If Mr. Firstman hit him— no, he wouldn't let himself be belted without trying to defend himself. He opened and closed his sweating hands.

"Get out of here!"

"What?"

"Get out of my sight! I can't stand your lying face. Go on, out of here. You're suspended, as of now. We don't want people like you in our school. And if you don't learn how to tell the truth you're going to be expelled as well. You go home and stay there till we call you and your parents to school."

Marcus dug out his jacket from his locker jammed with books and sneakers and old debris. He kicked the door shut, and gave it an extra kick to vent his feelings. The halls were empty as he hurried from the building.

He was walking toward his house when he saw Dorrity and Phillips and Flo waiting for him on the other side near the doughnut shop. He crossed the street against traffic, as Dorrity motioned to him urgently.

"Young Rosenbloom," Phillips said mockingly. Dorrity put his arm around Marcus's shoulder.

"They had you in there a long time, Marcus. They didn't try to pin anything on you, did they? You should have run."

Marcus had the uncomfortable impression that Dorrity was scared. His mouth looked pinched and he kept looking past Marcus. They all pressed around him.

"Did Firstman see us?" Phillips said, dropping his mocking manner. "When he came out of the building, we were out of sight. He didn't see us, did he?"

"He saw you under the stairwell," Marcus said, and then he corrected himself. "I think he saw you." It was important that he get everything right. "At least he said your names."

"You told him our names!" Phillips exclaimed. "Oh, this is the end!" He put his hands to his head. "If I get expelled my father is going to kill me."

"And what about me?" Dorrity said. "If my mother even hears drugs—" He broke off. "Let's not panic. Let's hear everything that Marcus has to say before we start jumping off a bridge."

"There's nothing to say." Phillips looked hatefully at Marcus. "He's already told everything. He's a fat, dumb kid. I never trusted him."

"I didn't say anything," Marcus said loudly, meeting Phillips's eyes. "Not a word." He wished it had been Phillips sitting in the office all day, being yelled at by Mr. Firstman. "I didn't talk," he repeated in a choked voice.

"I knew," Dorrity said, patting his back. "I knew it all the time!" There was relief in his voice. "Marcus won't blab, I said. And we've got nothing to worry about because The Hitter's got nothing on us. He's just guessing, throwing out names, isn't that right?"

"He's got the roach," Marcus said.

"The roach!" Dorrity turned on Phillips savagely. "I thought you said you got rid of it!"

"I thought I did," Phillips said weakly. "He came down too fast, I didn't think—"

"You should have swallowed it, or thrown it outside." There was contempt in Dorrity's voice. He turned back to Marcus. "Stay cool. So The Hitter's got the roach. Somebody threw it on the floor, that's all you know. You don't know who it was. You weren't looking, and when you looked they ran too fast, right?"

Marcus nodded dumbly. He was sweating again.

"Say it was a black kid if you have to," Phillips said cynically. "That's why you couldn't recognize him. They'll believe that. And if that doesn't work, we'll think of something else." His voice was jaunty again. "Okay, young Rosenbloom?" He gave Marcus's arm a quick squeeze. "Don't let us down."

"He said he'd expel me from school if I didn't tell him who you were," Marcus said.

"Don't believe that crap," Dorrity said. "He's just trying to scare you. He'll scare the hell out of you, then give you a warning and let you go. If it was

Phillips and me, though, it would be really bad news."

"You're young," Flo said reassuringly to Marcus. "They don't bother with the new kids, but if these guys get expelled, they'll never let them back in." Her arm around Dorrity's waist, she gave Marcus a wide, warm smile.

"What's the matter with those other boys?" his mother said that night after he'd told her what had happened. "They ran off and left you! A fine thing." Marcus had thought of waiting till the school got in touch with Sally before saying anything, but then decided that would be even worse. It was better to tell her and get it over with. She was upset. That was the really bad part of it. If he could have kept her out of it . . . but how?

"I don't understand your getting involved with something like this," she said. "Granted that you weren't smoking. Why were you even there? I only wish Bill wasn't gone. Maybe he could make some sense of this business. I can't."

Marcus shook his head, feeling worse and worse. He felt suddenly hungry, hollow with hunger, famished, and at the same time the thought of food made him slightly nauseated. He didn't finish his supper. Talking with his mother left him feeling miserable, as guilty as if he'd really done something wrong. In the back of his mind, too, was the weight of knowing that Dorrity hadn't said he'd step forward and clear everything up.

To make himself feel better he went out and tried calling Neal Renfrew on the North Side again, dreaming that with this one phone call he would find his father, or how to get in touch with him. God! That would turn the day around. That would make everything right! What had happened in school would dwindle to an insignificant event.

The phone rang twice and then was picked up. "Yes?" It was a man's rough voice. "Who the hell's waking me up?"

"Neal Renfrew?"

"That's right. Who is this?"

"I—I'm looking for my fa—is George Renfrew there?"

"Christ! A man works all day and can't get his sleep without some fool thing going on. Who'd you say you want?"

"George Renfrew."

"Never heard of him!" And the phone was hung up, the click echoing in Marcus's head like a slap in the face.

TWELVE

MR. FIRSTMAN had ordered Marcus to stay home, but the following morning a telephone call ordered him back to school. No, not to school exactly, but to the office, where he was told to stay. He wasn't allowed to attend classes. As if just his presence could contaminate the other students, he was isolated, condemned to sit in the glass-enclosed outer office where Mrs. Paoletti reigned. There, the notorious dope fiend, Marcus Rosenbloom, safely sanitized, was the center of attention of the passing throngs on the other side of the glass wall. He hid his concern under an assumed bravado—cool and casual. The Dorrity look. The Dorrity manner of total relaxation. If they wanted him to sit in the office, he didn't care. He'd sit here as long as they liked.

He crossed one leg over the other, flung his arms along the back of the bench. He pursed his mouth in a soundless whistle. He was innocent. He clung to his innocence, wrapping himself in it, reminding himself that he'd done nothing wrong, pushing down the anxious, guilty feelings that grew stronger the longer he sat there.

The black hat was on his head again. He had

gotten it wet, pounded it, sat on it, and jammed it
into his back pocket. The brim was broken, the once
lovely white feather was matted and gray and sat on
Marcus's head like a droopy bird. The principal saw
that hat and shook his head, as did Mr. Firstman,
and a few of the teachers who happened into the
office, but nobody told him to remove it.

Kids passed, some of them giving him friendly
salutes, others looking away as if they'd never seen
him. He overheard snatches of conversation. "That's
the kid who was busted for smoking pot . . . The first
one they ever grabbed in school . . . Yeah, that fat
one with the funny hat . . ."

Vivian passed and smiled. Flo and Barb went by,
their heads together, turning away at the last minute,
apparently not seeing him. Kids from his other classes
streamed by, but never Dorrity, Phillips, or Bisner.
Only Bernie came to see him in the office. He stood
inside, looking around, nervous and ill at ease. "I don't
have much time," he said.

"I won't be here long," Marcus said. "They've made
a mistake. I didn't do anything."

"That's what I told my parents," Bernie said, "but
my father said he doesn't want me to see you anymore."

"What!"

"He says where there's smoke, there's fire. My smart
sister stuck up for you, though."

"She did, really? Vivian did?" He felt a glad
warmth around his heart.

"Sure. She told my father when a friend's in trouble
you stick by them. But everybody knows that. It's just

like the time you broke your finger and your mother wasn't home, and I went to the doctor with you. My idea is that you stick by your friends, no matter what."

Of course, in all this Bernie was letting Marcus know that *he* hadn't stuck by his friendship to Bernie the way Bernie had stuck by him. "It's good to have true friends," Bernie said, and then turning the knife a little, "even *dumb* friends."

True friends. Marcus had been thinking a lot about that. He knew that Bernie was his true friend. But so was Dorrity. It would have been stupid for Dorrity to step forward now and get himself into deep trouble. It was better all around that he, Marcus, was up front. What could they do to him? Bawl him out some more, scare him, give him a warning? The worst they could do was keep him out of class for a few days. Well, he could take that without too much trouble. If Dorrity was in his place, Marcus wouldn't let him down. He wasn't going to let Dorrity down now. The whole thing had to blow over because it was stupid to keep him here when he hadn't done anything.

A while after Bernie had left, Mrs. Paoletti told Marcus to go to Mr. Firstman's office. Marcus entered, telling himself that a lecture and some more yelling weren't going to kill him. Because after that, Firstman would tell him to return to classes. By now he must have realized that Marcus had been telling him the simple truth, so there was nothing to be done.

Sitting at his desk Mr. Firstman didn't look up, nor did he ask Marcus to sit down. He had a piece of paper in front of him that he looked at as he told Marcus in a flat voice that he would have a hearing before Dr. Holley, the Superintendent of Schools, at a future date, and "as of right now, I'm turning you over to the police."

Marcus swallowed hard. His mouth dried out and his knees trembled. For a wild moment he thought it was Mr. Firstman's sadistic idea of a joke.

"What's your mother's phone number at work?"

Marcus shook his head dumbly. He couldn't remember it. His brain was blank.

Mr. Firstman called Mrs. Paoletti on the intercom. "Get me Mrs. Rosenbloom's number at work."

Marcus's head was in a whirl. While Mr. Firstman dialed his mother he concentrated on the framed diplomas on the wall—thick white paper with gold embossed words, framed in black. The words, unreadable, melted in front of his eyes. As from a great distance he heard Mr. Firstman saying, "Mrs. Rosenbloom? Yes, this is Mr. Firstman at Columbus School." Then he went on in the same flat voice, explaining that the drug laws of the state had been broken by Marcus, and for the school to delay any longer would make them party to the crime.

"What crime!" he heard his mother exclaim over the phone, but he couldn't catch what else she said. His mind swept wildly from thinking that it didn't matter —nothing was really going to happen—to the conviction that this was the end. Once the police got him they'd not only remove him from school but would put him in prison as well.

Half an hour later, a fat soft-spoken policeman placed Marcus in the back seat of his patrol car with the doors locked from the outside and a bulletproof partition between him and the front seat. He was driven through the city to the new Public Safety Building on Court Street, where he was handed over to the Juvenile Protection Division on the fifth floor. There he was put into a tiny windowless cubicle by another policeman. Nothing was said to him. The door wasn't locked, but he sat as if bound in the room's single metal chair beside the square metal table, unable to control his wild feeling that when they returned they would strap him to the table and beat a confession out of him.

Suddenly he pictured his father in a similar situation. His father had been through it all—leg irons, and truth serums, and being kept in "tiger cages" in the ground under a blazing tropical sun. And never once had he cracked.

Remember, his father said, *when they start beating you, don't ever betray your comrades in arms!* He put his big rough hand on Marcus's shoulder . . .

The fantasy faded. Marcus couldn't hold onto it. He jumped at the sound of footsteps outside the cubicle, but the door remained closed. He sat there for what seemed like hours. Footsteps passed back and forth, he heard the murmur of voices and the clicking of a typewriter. Then, at last, the door opened and there was his mother looking upset and angry, as close to tears as he'd ever seen her. "They say you can come out now, Marcus." She put her arms around him briefly. A mustached policeman sat at a typewriter behind a low wooden railing. There were forms to be filled out, questions to be answered. "The boy's name?" the policeman asked his mother. As if Marcus were too young or too stupid to answer. "The boy's address? The boy's age? The boy's father's name?"

In a curt voice Sally told the policeman that she was the one who assumed full responsibility for anything involving her son. The policeman glanced up at a lieutenant who had come out of an inner office and was standing over him, hands behind his back, listening. It was the lieutenant who told Sally that because of Marcus's age, his case would be turned over to the Family Court authorities. "We will release him into your custody on your signature that he will appear in Family Court when so ordered."

Sally nodded. "What do I sign?"

The policeman pushed a sheet of paper in front of her.

At no time did either man look at Marcus or raise his voice in accusation or probing question. To them, it seemed, this was routine, cut and dried, questions and answers with which they were bored.

"The school—?" Sally said.

The lieutenant shook his head. "The school will hold their own hearing." He glanced at Marcus. "These crazy kids. You have my sympathy. You ought to talk straight to your son. I understand he's not being cooperative with the school authorities. Family Court will hear about that, of course. You might remind your son that the judge has got the authority to send him to Stony Point Rehabilitation Center for up to two years."

Marcus's ears rang. Two years in a reform school.

"Luckily," the lieutenant went on, "Family Court is more interested in rehabilitation in the home environment, if possible. Confession is always a good first step in rehabilitation."

"I don't know why my son has to be put through this kind of ordeal," Sally burst out. "He wasn't smoking marijuana. He's never broken the law. He's not a criminal, so why—"

Fingering the big buckle of his gun belt, the lieutenant said, "Drug abuse, lady, is rampant in the schools. You read the papers, don't you? Everybody's doing it. It's an epidemic, it's reaching down to the grade schools. Little kids. Kindergarten kids are already being corrupted. You want those kids to grow up to be dope fiends? We've got to get the pushers."

"Are you accusing my son of being a pusher?" Sally stood tall, clutching her shoulder purse.

"I didn't say that. But this boy knows more than he's telling. Drugs are poison. If this boy were mine, I'd get the truth out of him, and fast. And for his own good."

"If my son did something wrong, he should be punished, but no one should be punished for refusing to tell on someone else." His mother's voice was low, level, harsh with anger.

The lieutenant sighed. "Every kid that's ever been caught red-handed has his mother believing he's innocent. Open your eyes and face facts, lady, and stop fighting us!" His voice had risen.

Marcus pushed in front of his mother. "My mother doesn't know anything about this. Don't yell at her."

He was scared out of his mind. The man could have pulled out his gun and killed him on the spot. But nothing was happening the way he imagined. Instead of beating him, the lieutenant gave him a bored look, turned his back and instructed the mustached policeman to show him and Sally the way out.

A week later Marcus and Sally were summoned downtown to the County Court Building for an interview with the Intake Office of Family Court. They were at the office promptly at two-thirty, but were told by a woman behind a high desk that the Intake Officer was detained at an "important meeting." For over an hour they sat in the waiting room, reading old copies of *Time* magazine.

Finally they were called. The Intake Officer was a woman who reminded Marcus at once of a teacher he'd had in Prescott School. She wore a flowered yellow dress, yellow earrings, and pointed rhinestone glasses. For fifteen minutes she lectured him on the evils of drugs and the shortsightedness of the younger generation who were coddled, indulged, and spoiled. "The aim of Family Court is not to punish those who stray," she said, "but to educate. You're not going to do this again, are you, Marcus? You understand how wrong drugs are, and how bad they are for you?"

"Yes," Marcus said. "But I wasn't smoking."

"He does well in school, Mrs. Rosenbloom?" she said, turning to Sally. "Have you had any trouble with him before?"

"Marcus is a wonderful boy," Sally said. "Cooperative and helpful, and never in any kind of trouble. As for this thing, being here—he is a victim of circumstances. He wasn't smoking that cigarette."

"I see you're a single-parent family," she said, ignoring Sally's statement. "And there are no siblings." She made these remarks sound vaguely accusatory.

"I spend all my free time with my son," Sally said. "I have to work, of course."

"I understand," the Intake Officer said, peering down at her notes. "Are you having financial problems? What other problems do you have?"

"No problems," Sally said. "We get along perfectly, don't we, Marcus?"

"Yes," he said. He plucked at the knees of his jeans, feeling dimly guilty, because he knew they didn't get along perfectly. He felt responsible for his mother's being here and the way his mother was making up to the Intake Officer, letting the woman call her Mrs. Rosenbloom. It was so unlike Sally.

The Intake Officer glanced out the window, fingering her earring. "You're not going to do this again, Marcus? You're off drugs now, aren't you? You realize they're wrong, and you've learned your lesson."

"I—no—" He started to protest his innocence once again, but was immediately aware that it didn't matter what he said. Ever since The Hitter had come creeping down the stairs intent on catching someone —anyone—smoking pot, everyone in authority had had his mind made up about him. Marcus had been caught, therefore he was guilty.

"If you hear of anyone using drugs, you'd tell us, Marcus? You don't have to be involved. Just call me and I'll inform the proper authorities. There may even be a reward for useful information." She smiled at Sally. "I'm sure you'll be glad to hear, Mrs. Rosenbloom, that I've decided on the basis of this interview that Marcus does not have to appear in Family Court."

"Does *not*?" Sally said.

"That's right. I'm sure he's going to be all right. His records will go into the dead file. Of course, you want to stay out of trouble, Marcus," she said.

"He will," Sally said. "Oh yes, he will do that."

"The file is dead," the Intake Officer said, "but then, it's always there, isn't it? A juvenile offender file." She gave Marcus a soft, vague smile, quite a nice smile. "Now you go home and be a good boy."

"Yes," Marcus said.

"Thank you," Sally said. "Thank you very much." Outside on the front steps she hugged Marcus. "No court appearance! That's good. That's wonderful. And no record, not really. I think they throw away those dead files every couple of years. Now I need a drink," she said. "God! This involvement with the law. I have so many horrible fears—that they'll take you away, say I'm not a fit mother, put you into an institution." She shuddered. "That's why I put up with that hypocritical business of letting myself be called Mrs. Rosenbloom. If that woman had known I've brought you up unmarried and alone—I tell you, I shudder to think of it."

"I'm sorry, Sally." He was sorry that she'd been involved, that for his sake she'd had to agree with everything that woman had said. As for himself, it was hard to believe that anything real had happened. He had imagined himself defending his innocence, being vindicated, but even the Intake Officer's decision that he didn't have to appear in Family Court didn't mean she believed he was innocent. She had been vaguely like an indulgent relative—be a good boy and don't do it again and I'll let you off this time. But what did that and her vague threats about the dead file have to do with what had really happened?

Sally put her arm through his. "Now that it's over, don't you feel better? I do!"

Arm in arm, they crossed Court Street, passed the Court House, and walked down Division Street to a restaurant where Sally said she would treat him to an ice cream soda. "Two down, and one to go," she said as they entered the restaurant. "I can't believe the school hearing can be any worse than this."

THIRTEEN

THE HEARING before the Superintendent of Schools was held in the old Board of Education Building, the converted red brick West Broadway School with its tall windows and creaky, shiny wooden floors. The hearing room was downstairs in what was once the music room. To Marcus's surprise both Phillips and Dorrity were there. Seeing them, he felt at once cheered and anxious. What did their presence mean? Had they admitted their guilt and spoken out about his innocence? Had they realized that things had gone farther than any of them had expected?

Dorrity's mother, who had the same sandy hair as Dorrity, was with him holding his hand. It gave Marcus a start to see Dorrity sitting so docilely next to his mother, wearing a tie and suit, somehow changed, controlled, even diminished. It made him uneasy. Dorrity, who had been his hero, seemed hemmed in, smaller, less wonderful, ordinary. Marcus kept glancing his way, looking for the reassurance of Dorrity's bold unquenchable smile. But Dorrity didn't appear aware of him.

The hearing began when Dr. Holley, the Superintendent of Schools, seated himself at the long wooden table and called on Mr. Firstman to begin. The vice principal took the seat next to Dr. Holley's. He adjusted his cuffs, then slid around so that he was facing Dr. Holley. Clearing his throat, he spoke in a low, unemphasized voice, totally different from the dramatic tone taken with Marcus in his office. ". . . and on that Monday, as I was checking the halls, I smelled a distinct ropy odor near the gymnasium . . ."

Sitting at the farther end of the wooden table, Sally behind him on the other side of the low wooden railing, Marcus could see through the windows. Cars were rushing past on the overpass. And through the corner windows he saw the firehouse across the street and the long rows of auto lots that lined West Broadway.

Each time Mr. Firstman mentioned Marcus by name, Dr. Holley looked over at Marcus. He was bald, with an oval face, like a yellow egg wearing large black-rimmed glasses. The boy in Marcus would have liked to disappear, to slide under this long table and slip away between the legs of all these grownups, the way he'd been able to slip and slide in crowds as a little kid. He sat up, reminding himself he had nothing to hide. He had only to tell the truth. If everyone told the exact truth then they'd know he had done nothing wrong.

The Superintendent was paying close attention to Mr. Firstman's testimony. He was now saying that he'd seen two other boys along with Marcus, but by the time he got there, he found only Marcus.

"And the marijuana butt," Dr. Holley prompted.

"Yes, and the marijuana cigarette," Mr. Firstman

said. "I knew it was marijuana, I had smelled it from above. A strong ropy smell," he repeated.

It amazed Marcus the number of people involved in this hearing. He'd had the same feeling at police headquarters. So many grown people involved in kids' affairs. In the hearing room, besides the parents, there was the Superintendent, who was judge and jury, Mr. Firstman, a blonde woman Marcus couldn't identify, and a male stenographer who took down every word on a steno machine.

Dr. Holley, caressing his shining bald head, asked Mr. Firstman to tell him again exactly how he'd found Marcus.

"He was crouched down under the stairwell, with the roach in his hand as if he were trying to hide it, or rub it out."

"No," Marcus said. "I never touched it. I didn't even know it was there."

"Please," Dr. Holley said in his deep, resonant voice, a voice fitted for sincere roles, "this is not the way we conduct things. You'll have your turn to talk, Marcus."

Marcus sat up, pressing his back against the chair. He stared at Mr. Firstman. Tell the truth, he commanded mentally. The truth. You know you picked up that roach from the floor.

Mr. Firstman went back to the other two boys. Yes, he'd glimpsed them, but only dimly, he was unable to make a positive identification. However, he'd felt quite sure they were James Dorrity and Donald Phillips. Marcus, of course, could make a positive identification, but he had received no cooperation from the boy. As he said this, he thinned his mouth and glanced stonily in Marcus's direction, as if his lack of cooperation had been a personal affront.

"Thank you, Mr. Firstman," Dr. Holley said when he finished speaking. "I appreciate your testimony. I know you have a very full schedule, and I hope this hearing hasn't taken too much of your time."

"You're welcome, Dr. Holley, but I must add no time spent in your office is wasted." The two men nodded gravely to one another as if they'd never met before this day, as if Dr. Holley wasn't Mr. Firstman's boss, as if it wasn't Dr. Holley himself who had hired Mr. Firstman, and Dr. Holley himself who could also fire Mr. Firstman if he so desired.

"Mrs. Morrison, please," Dr. Holley said, and the blonde woman stood and drew a little sheaf of papers out of a tan leather briefcase. At the back of the room the radiator pipes clicked, as a wave of heat rolled into the room, and Marcus felt stifled, choking.

"Dr. Holley, for the benefit of the others in this room," Mrs. Morrison said, "I want to briefly state my qualifications. I am presently the senior chemist with the Medical Examiner's Office assigned to the police laboratory. I previously taught chemistry and biology at the college level. I was a toxicologist for Broome County. I was a chemist for the government . . ."

She spoke in a clipped brisk voice. She wore a fuzzy hat and glasses with dark eyeshades clipped to the top. She had on a brown jumper and a yellow jersey and looked only at the papers spread out on the wooden table. When Dr. Holley asked her a question, she ignored it and continued talking in the same clipped brisk manner.

"In this envelope—" she held up a small brown envelope, "is Evidence Number 037043, which I was asked to analyze. There was 0.014 gram of plant material. This material was put under a microscope for analysis. I then took the material and ashed it—"

"Asked it?" Dr. Holley interrupted.

The chemist continued talking. "I then reexamined it for characteristic hairs that belong only to cannabis. I then added hydrochloric acid to watch the effervescence. I then took some of the material in a small vial and added a chemical agent . . . characteristic purple color . . . positive identification as *Cannabis sativa* . . ."

"Dr. Holley—"

To Marcus's surprise Sally was standing. "Dr. Holley, I'd like to ask Mrs. Morrison to translate for the rest of us the amount of plant material she said she found into some measure we could understand better."

"Well—ah—certainly. Mrs. Morrison—"

"There are 28.35 grams to an ounce," the chemist said. "The amount of plant material involved was approximately one milligram."

"What would a regular cigarette weigh?" Sally asked.

Everyone looked at her. Marcus squirmed, but at the same time he felt proud. Sally wasn't scared of anybody.

"I don't know," the chemist said. She pushed her

glasses more firmly up on her nose. "Perhaps half a gram. Perhaps the amount of plant material involved here was about one-fiftieth of a whole cigarette."

"One-fiftieth," Sally repeated. "Thank you." She looked at Dr. Holley. "I can barely imagine one-fiftieth of a cigarette, can you, Dr. Holley?"

His only response was a tightening of his lips.

"Thank you, Mrs. Morrison," Dr. Holley said. "I appreciate your cooperation and taking your valuable time." He waited for her to leave before calling Donald Phillips. Marcus twisted around. Phillips was sitting between his parents. His father, a trim, well-barbered man, looked at Marcus with a cold expression. Phillips stood up, passed in front of his parents and around the low wooden railing. He looked unnaturally neat in a sports jacket and tie, and his hair slicked back. Marcus was made aware of the way he himself was dressed, in jeans and an ordinary shirt, sloppy compared to the neat appearance of his friends.

"Sit here, Donald," Dr. Holley said, pointing to the chair next to him. "Now then, Donald, you know why you're here. Mr. Firstman says he saw you leaving the scene on the day he caught Marcus Rosenbloom with marijuana."

Marcus was jolted. Dr. Holley had spoken as if already convinced of his guilt. But wasn't this hearing supposed to determine the facts?

"No, sir, he couldn't have seen me," Phillips said, his hands clasped easily in front of him. "I happened to be in the lunchroom at the time."

"The lunchroom?" Dr. Holley rubbed his bald head.

"I believe we're talking about the morning, before first period."

"Yes, sir. I happened to miss breakfast that morning. My mom wasn't feeling good, so I left the house without having had anything to eat. When I got to school I thought I'd better get myself a container of milk. I know Mrs. Oliver who works in the cafeteria and I thought she'd sell me a container of milk." Phillips told his story with such an air of conviction and easy assurance that Marcus felt that if he didn't know better he'd believe Phillips, too. It was all so smooth. And every word was a lie.

Dr. Holley next asked Phillips if he knew Marcus. "Are you friends?"

Phillips shook his head. He didn't look at Marcus. "I've seen him around school, but he's not my friend." And then he added, "He's just a seventh-grade kid. I'm in ninth grade. We don't have anything in common."

The betrayal was deep and heavy in Marcus's gut. Phillips was lying, but then maybe they'd never been friends. Not real friends the way he was with Dorrity. He watched Phillips sit down between his parents. Then Dorrity was called, and Marcus's eyes switched to him. He leaned forward, eagerly waiting for Dorrity to speak. Dorrity would clear things up. Dorrity would back up his story. Dorrity would tell the truth, even if it hurt, because Dorrity didn't think of his own skin first.

The questions were the same that had been asked Phillips. "Were you in the stairwell on Monday morning?"

"No, sir," Dorrity said. "I was in the boys lav."

"Which one?"

"Third floor."

"Did anyone else see you there?"

Dorrity shrugged. "I suppose so. I wasn't thinking about it." His face was pale.

Dr. Holley looked at him severely. "Have you ever smoked marijuana?"

Dorrity hesitated, then said, "Yes. A couple of times."

"In school?"

"No, sir!" Dorrity said. "I wouldn't be that stupid."

"Somebody apparently was that stupid," Dr. Holley said dryly.

When Dorrity was finished and passed by, Marcus closed his eyes. He didn't want to see Dorrity, or hear anything. The pain he felt, the sickness that made him want to double up and press his fingers against his eyes and ears were for this boy he had once thought to be better than anyone else. Dorrity, too, had denied any friendship with Marcus!

Marcus was the last witness. At first his mouth was so dry he had to work the words out around his tongue, licking his lips to get a little moisture. His friends' betrayal still rang in his ears. His friends had lied. Mr. Firstman had seen what he wanted to see, and Dr. Holley was convinced of Marcus's guilt. He answered the questions briefly, without hope. Where did he live? Did he like school? Was he happy? Were there teachers he didn't like?

Yes, he liked school. He liked his teachers. Even if,

sometimes, he didn't like them, he said he knew they were all trying to do something good for him and the other kids.

Then the Superintendent was asking him about that morning below the stairs. What was he doing there, at the bottom of the stairs?

"I was looking for a friend."

"Did you find your friend?"

Marcus wet his lips. "Yes," he said at last.

"Was there anyone else there?"

"Yes."

"How many people were there?" Dr. Holley asked in a relaxed, gentle tone.

"Two people, besides me."

"Then Mr. Firstman was correct in saying he saw two boys running away?"

"Yes," Marcus said. The truth—he would tell the truth.

"Why were you looking for this friend?"

"I wanted to show him my father's name."

"Your father's name was on the slip of paper that you say fell?"

Marcus nodded. The Superintendent seemed to really understand. He began to dream that Dr. Holley cared. He reminded Marcus of somebody, he didn't know who exactly, but it was somebody he liked. He began to imagine that he would tell Dr. Holley his father's name, and Dr. Holley would know his father, or his father's family. Maybe they grew up together and were friends. And when he knew that Marcus was George Renfrew's son, he'd know that he could never lie, or use drugs, or get other people in trouble.

"Why did you want to show your friend your father's name?"

Marcus turned so his eyes met the Superintendent's. "I thought he could help me find my father."

"Don't you know where your father is?"

Behind him a chair creaked. "No," he said.

Every question about his father made him feel surer about Dr. Holley. His face was kindly, his eyes behind the glasses attentive, drooping a little in the corners. Yes, he really cared. He understood how important it was for Marcus to find his father, and how smoking grass had been the farthest thing from Marcus's mind.

"Did your friend know where your father is?"

"I didn't have a chance to ask him."

"Was your friend smoking?" The turn back to the question of marijuana startled Marcus.

"I think so."

"You're not sure?"

"I don't know, I wasn't thinking about it."

"Will you tell us the names of those two boys, Marcus?"

The cords in Marcus's neck strained to keep his head and eyes from turning toward Dorrity.

"Are those boys in this room?"

Marcus twisted in his chair. The Superintendent's face had turned flat as an oval dish, features pressed down, his eyes like hard flat watermelon seeds. "Will you tell us their names, Marcus?" he repeated. "Or point them out? Will you be cooperative, Marcus? Everything points to you as the guilty party, but

156

cooperation would mean a lot. I have to decide this case, to judge, weigh every factor. I have to decide who is going to be punished and to what degree."

Marcus couldn't move his eyes from those steady flat eyes. The muscles in his neck ached, his head felt rigid as if it were fixed on a steel rod.

"Their names, Marcus. Are they in this room? Now is your chance to speak up." All Marcus could see were those eyes demanding that he answer. "This is your last chance," the Superintendent said. Marcus pushed back the chair, turned, half rose to his feet. He saw them all for a moment like a mural on the wall: Dorrity looking at the floor. Phillips with a half smile, glancing out the window. His own mother, her eyes fixed on him. What did the expression on her face mean? What was she thinking? Did she want him to name Phillips and Dorrity? Why should he go on protecting them anymore? His throat ached, thinking of Dorrity's betrayal. "No, he's no friend of mine, he's just a kid around school," Dorrity had said in answer to one of the Superintendent's questions. Marcus gripped the arm of his chair. They'd lied, put the blame on him, all to save their own skins. He could save his skin, too. He had only to tell the utter and complete truth.

"Will you answer the question?" Dr. Holley said. "Are they in this room?"

Marcus glanced at Sally, whose eyes never left his. He shook his head. "I can't. I can't be the one to get other people in trouble. I told you everything about myself. I told you the truth. Won't you believe me?"

"You aren't going to tell us their names?"

Marcus shook his head.

"Do you have anything else to say?"

"I wasn't smoking. I've never smoked marijuana. That's the truth."

Dr. Holley scribbled something on his pad. In the silence of the hearing room only the scratch of his pen was heard. Then he rose to his feet. "This hearing is over. I thank you all for coming. Mrs. Dorrity, Mr. and Mrs. Phillips, Mrs. Rosenbloom, I'll let you know my decision on your sons by mail." He gathered his papers into a heap and stuffed them hastily into a leather briefcase and left at once.

Was that it? Was it over? When Marcus turned, Dorrity and Phillips and their parents were already gone. Marcus joined his mother. What would she say now? He had a chance to make things easier for himself and had thrown it away. "Sally—?" he said uncertainly.

She took his arm and embraced him. There was a fierce brightness in her eyes. "What you said, what you did—it was so good. I was so proud of my son, Marcus."

FOURTEEN

HANGING AROUND the apartment waiting for the letter from Dr. Holley that would decide his fate, Marcus had too much time on his hands. The only good thing that happened was that without even trying he was losing weight. At first he'd been so agitated that his stomach had felt full all the time, and now he just wasn't hungry.

One afternoon, bored silly with his own company and with nothing to think about except why the Superintendent was taking so long to make up his mind, Marcus wandered over to school. Standing outside he watched the kids streaming out, and almost at once caught sight of Dorrity. He'd thought he wouldn't have any feeling about him anymore, but his stomach jumped. He'd made Dorrity into something special, a hero. But Dorrity had never been a hero, just another kid, perhaps cleverer than most at getting other people to do things for him. He wasn't a dozen feet from Marcus, standing alone. Dorrity raised his hand. He seemed about to smile, to say something. Marcus hesitated; despite everything, part of him was still attracted to the older boy. Then at the last moment he turned and walked away.

"Hey, Marc." It was Bernie, and Vivian was with

him. Marcus hadn't been to their house in weeks. Now, suddenly he felt almost overwhelmed at seeing his friends again. Vivian rushed up and put her arm through his, and then both of them, Bernie and Vivian, asked him a dozen questions about the hearing and what he was doing and if he thought Dr. Holley had believed him.

Marcus kicked at a pebble. "You know what I think—I think if he believed me, then it makes Mr. Firstman out to be a liar, which he is, saying he caught me with the roach in my hand. But who's going to believe me over him?"

"I do," Vivian said stoutly.

"Me, too," Bernie said.

"Don't get down in the mouth over this," Vivian advised. "You never know," she said. "It might turn out to be the best thing that ever happened to you. Sometimes the worst things turn out to be better than you ever expected."

"Don't be an idiot," Bernie said. "It's the worst thing that ever happened to Marcus, so how can it turn out good?"

Marcus said that whatever happened he wasn't worried. But beneath his words he felt how different things really were. Standing there in the late afternoon sunshine with his friends, scuffing leaves and laughing at their bickering, he felt separated from them. It was the same feeling he'd had most sharply in the hearing room when the hearing was finally over and he'd sat alone for a moment at one end of the long shiny table, betrayed by those he called his friends, used by the adults who should have cared

160

about him. He felt separated even from himself—the dreamer with his great expectations. To the very end he had thought he'd be rescued. Dorrity would speak the truth; Dr. Holley would see through the lie; his father would break down the doors and speak out in his behalf. And none of it had happened.

That same night he went up on the roof of his building and looked out over the city. He could see the new construction below and the glitter of lights on the highway, and in the distance the blue bridge lights arcing up over the river. He walked along the perimeter of the roof. There was a place he could throw a leg over and hop down to the next roof. Sitting astride the wall, he saw in a window a mother bending over a baby in a crib. And then in another window, like a picture on a TV screen, he saw Willis Pierce sitting at a table, and across from him a man, perhaps his father, talking, his skinny arms going up and down. Willis sat with his chin in his hand, listening to the man, really listening and not saying a word. Marcus had never seen Willis so quiet and attentive. It gave Marcus an odd feeling, as if he were seeing Willis in a secret way, a way he wasn't supposed to, but one that was more truthful than all the other ways he'd known Willis before. A pain, like hunger, spread through Marcus's body and then he felt a hollowness so deep in him that he thought he'd never lose it. His father, his own father! There was Willis Pierce with *his* father, and here was he, Marcus Rosenbloom, alone.

*　　*　　*

"George Renfrew?" A woman's voice answered Marcus's ring. "There's nobody here by that name!" The phone clicked.

On the couch with his legs slung over the back, Marcus was dialing every Renfrew in the telephone book, one by one, and he was having no luck at all. There were no Renfews listed where his father had once lived on Raymond Street.

"Who? What number do you want?"

"This is Renfrew's, but there's no George here, honey."

"Renfrew? Renfrew? Oh, Renfrew! No, they don't live here any more. Call information for their new number."

One by one he crossed out the Renfrews. Then— one time a woman answered. "One minute." He could hear her yelling. "George, one of your friends is on the phone. Hurry up!"

Marcus's heart nearly stopped.

"Hello?"

"I'm looking for George Renfrew," he said.

"That's me—Georgie. Who's this? This isn't Wally, is it?"

Marcus didn't answer. Georgie was a kid, just like him.

"Hey, who is this? Sal? Robby? Why don't you answer? Hey, did you call me up for something, or what?"

"Sorry—" Marcus managed to say and then hung up.

It was only later, when he'd gone through all the Renfrews in the book and none of them had yielded any information, that he thought to call Georgie Renfrew back and ask him his father's name. It was Peter.

The results were disappointing, but Marcus wasn't discouraged for long. He felt that for the first time in his life he was doing something important, really searching for his father. He had never thought it would be as easy as placing a phone call anyway.

The day the letter from Dr. Holley came, Sally was at work. Although it was addressed to her, Marcus opened the letter. The paper and the envelope were both thick and creamy, the message typewritten in elegant cursive script. For a moment the words didn't seem real to Marcus. "Dear Mrs. Rosenbloom, I have taken the matter of your son Marcus under serious consideration . . . have given much thought . . . not a matter to be treated lightly . . . believe me, I am deeply concerned . . ."

Marcus skipped down the page, past the Superintendent's review of his school records and various test results. "Excellent intelligence . . . good ability to comprehend . . . high verbal ability . . . however I am concerned about his self-image . . . health record shows he is overweight . . . several minor disturbances . . . even before the incident with marijuana . . ."

At last the letter came to the point. "Your son denies having smoked; however, the vice principal found him with the remains of the cigarette in his hand. The evidence seems clear. Therefore, in the hope that he will be able to make a fresh start with new friends and new surroundings, I am expelling him from Columbus Junior High School, while at the same time recommending that he be enrolled in Bradford Junior High."

When she read the letter, Sally was upset and furious. "What good was the hearing? He might just as well have listened to Mr. Firstman's story and made up his mind from that. All this baloney about his being so concerned, caring so much. I don't believe a word of it! And now to send you to another school, all the way across the city—what's the point? What sense does that make?"

"It's all right," Marcus said. "Don't worry." Now that the letter had arrived, now that the stupid business was finally over and settled, he felt relieved, almost glad. It was a blow to be suspended from his own school, separated from friends he'd known for years and everything that was familiar. But the school that Dr. Holley had chosen for him appeared to Marcus to be some sort of omen. Bradford Junior High was on the North Side, near the Iron Works, where his father used to live. Could it be only blind chance that he was being sent there? The Superintendent could have sent him anywhere in the city, but he'd chosen the exact place where Marcus was planning to go next in his search for his father. That had to mean something. He was gripped with fresh excitement. It was only a matter of time now—things were coming together. Lines were converging. Roads were opening up. Even the meaningless events around his drug arrest were being turned into something important.

His first week in Bradford Junior High, Marcus

knew no one. Everything was different—routine, teachers, classmates. But the new school remained a blurred background to his excited, eager thoughts. Bradford Junior High was only ten blocks away from Canal Street, where his father's parents had once run a variety store; and somewhere nearby was Raymond Street, where his father had once lived.

He found Raymond Street easily enough, a short street composed of tumble-down, unpainted houses. But the house where his father had lived was gone and the empty lot was choked with rusty brown weeds. Nobody on the street knew anything about the Renfrews. Now the only lead remaining to Marcus was the old family variety store.

On Canal Street, he discovered there was only one variety store—Brampton's. It was situated on the first floor of a weathered, gray wooden building. One window was piled high with sun-bleached boxes of sneakers. Through the glass Marcus could see the cash register on the counter near the door. Bells tinkled when he opened the door and a large, worried-looking man appeared from the back of the store. "Yes? Can I help you?"

Marcus, a little uncomfortable because he wasn't buying anything, said he was looking for a family of people named Renfrew. "They used to own a store on this street, a store like this one—sort of a variety store."

"What about them?"

"My mother knew George Renfrew. I'm trying to find him."

"I can't help you."

"You can't help me?" Marcus repeated. The man shook his head. Marcus was scared. Again he had come up against a blank wall. What would he do now? He had felt so sure that there, at last, he would find a connection to his father. He knew there was no point in standing and staring at the man, but he couldn't make his feet turn toward the door. Once he left, what was left for him to do in the search for his father? "Do you know what store the Renfrews used to own?" he asked, without hope of an answer. "Do you know where it was?"

"Sure I know," the man said, sounding slightly irritated. "This is the store they used to own."

Marcus's heart jumped. "This store!"

"That's right. I bought this store from the Renfrews seven years ago, but I never saw them. They were in Texas, or some such place."

"Texas," Marcus said, fiddling nervously with a tray full of bright plastic yo-yos. Texas—he could never go to Texas. Even if he could, how would he find one man in that whole huge state. He blinked his eyes. "Texas," he said again. "Oh."

"You want to buy one of those yo-yos?" the man said. "I haven't got all day."

Marcus stuffed his hands into his pockets. "Did you know George Renfrew?"

The man shook his head. "I told you, sonny, I never knew any of them. We did all our business through the lawyers. And they charged plenty. Lawyers!"

The man fell silent. Marcus searched for something to say that would elicit another response from him.

Again he felt as if he were on the verge of something important—but Texas! If his father were in Texas . . . all at once he saw himself on the highway, thumbing a ride. Why not? Texas wasn't the other side of the world.

"My sister-in-law knows that whole family," the man went on.

"What?" Marcus pulled his imagination back from the highway, where he'd just been taking a ride with a big, brawny trucker.

"Marie Belco," the man said. He paused again.

Go on, Marcus thought. Go *on*.

"Lives over there on Spring Street," he said. "She's my wife's sister. She married a cousin of the Renfrews, Bruno Belco."

Bells tinkled and several people entered the store. "Yes?" the man said. "Can I help you?"

"Thank you!" Marcus said. "Thanks a million!" He flew out of the store. Belco on Spring Street! That had to be the lead he was looking for. He asked a woman the way to Spring Street, but then instead of going straight there, he stepped into a phone booth and flipped through the directory. There it was. Bruno Belco, 155 Spring Street, and the phone number. Marcus looked out at the traffic. He was excited and anxious at the same time. What if he called Mrs. Belco, and when she heard a kid asking questions she hung up? He tried deepening his voice. "Hello, Mrs. Belco, this is Marcus Rosenbloom," he thundered in the empty booth. "I'm a private investigator. I'm on a mission to find a man named George Renfrew." He cleared his throat, dropped a dime into the slot, and

167

dialed the Belco number. The phone rang once. Suddenly he was sure this was the wrong way to do things. He hung up and ran out.

The Belco house was on the corner of Spring Street, one side red shingles and the other gray shingles. A dog stood on the porch barking at Marcus. There was a large tree close to an upstairs enclosed porch, with slats up the tree like a ladder. Underneath the tree there was a car up on cinder blocks.

Marcus walked past the house, went around the block and came down Spring Street again, scared and excited, still not sure about going in there. He'd better go home and think about it some more. But he didn't want to go home. He wanted to know now about his father. It was frightening to realize that if Marie Belco couldn't or wouldn't tell him where he could find his father, or his father's family, he had nowhere else to turn.

He went around the block again, working out what he'd say, so the Belcos wouldn't be suspicious or mad at being bothered by a kid. As he went around the block a third time, he became aware that someone was following him. Looking over his shoulder he saw a boy on a bike, zigzagging from one side of the street to the other. Marcus stopped in front of the Belcos, put his hands in his pockets, took them out, wiped them on his pants, then went up on the Belco porch. The fat brown dog backed up, barking loudly, and behind him he heard the bike rider calling.

"Hey, who you looking for?" The boy had gotten off the bike and was coming up on the porch behind

Marcus. He had a big head, straw-colored hair, and wore a striped T-shirt. He ordered the fat dog to pipe down. "You want somebody here?" he asked Marcus.

"The Blechos," Marcus said, in his excitement getting the name wrong.

"Not Blech-o! *Bel*-co, like Bell Company. I'm Danny Belco. I've been watching every move you've made since you came down Spring Street. I bet you didn't know you were being watched. You went around the block three times. How come? Couldn't you find the house? Or are you casing the neighborhood?"

"I'm looking for Mrs. Belco," Marcus said.

"That's my mother." Danny led the way down the narrow side of the porch, past a refrigerator, and opened a rusting screen door, calling out, "Ma, there's a kid here to see you. Ma! Hey, Ma! I said there's a kid here to see you."

There was a silence, then the annoyed voice of Mrs. Belco. "I hear you, you don't have to yell." She appeared, hardly glancing at Marcus. "What are you bothering me for, Danny? What does that boy want? If he's selling anything, we don't want it. We get all the magazines we want, and we don't buy anything else."

Danny turned to Marcus. "What do you want? My mother doesn't want to buy anything."

"I'm not selling anything," Marcus said. "I just want to talk to you, Mrs. Belco."

"That's a sales pitch if I ever heard one," she said.

"No, Mrs. Belco," Marcus said quickly, "Mr.—uh—

169

the man at Brampton's Department Store sent me over."

"You sure? Okay, come on in and shut the door." She was a heavy-set woman with a puffy face, wearing blue jeans and green sneakers. "What is it, then?"

"I'm looking for a friend of my mother's," Marcus said. Mrs. Belco stared at him. "She works, so she asked me to find him," he said hurriedly. "They used to be close friends. Now she's lost touch with him."

Mrs. Belco frowned. "Do I know your mother? Who's this friend? What's this all got to do with me?"

"George Renfrew," Marcus said.

"Oh, him," she said. "I don't know much about him."

"That's the rich side of the family," Danny told Marcus. "We never see Cousin George, do we, Mom? He's got a big boat. And he flies all over. And he's never invited us on his boat once, has he, Mom?"

"Why don't you shut up, Danny," his mother said. "You know you've got a big mouth. Why don't you wait till I find out what's going on here." Turning to Marcus, she said, "Now why did you say you want to see George Renfrew? Never mind what you just heard. I didn't say I knew him, did I?"

Marcus, who could barely contain his excitement, told Mrs. Belco again about his mother's knowing George Renfrew from the old days, and their being friends, and then losing touch.

"I bet she was one of his girl friends. He had dozens of them," Mrs. Belco said. "Now how come your mother's sending her kid around on an errand like this?"

Marcus was sorry now he hadn't stayed outside and asked Danny his questions. Danny would have told him anything he wanted to know. "My mother works, and anyway I go to Bradford Junior High," Marcus said, "and I was in the neighborhood—"

Danny, listening with interest, said, "You in Bradford? I am, too. I never saw you there."

"I'm new," Marcus said. "This was my first week."

"You go to the same school as Danny, then," Mrs. Belco said, and as if this had settled something in her mind she told her son to get her the black and white address book from the telephone table. "It's in the little drawer, Danny. I'm going to give you George's address at his company," she explained to Marcus. "But that's all I'm going to do. Your mother can do her own talking and explaining, because I don't talk to George that much."

"Texas telephone calls must be expensive," Marcus said.

"Texas. Who said anything about Texas? He's not my cousin, anyway, he's my husband's cousin. I don't suppose it'll hurt anything if I give you his business address. He can't complain about that, can he?"

"He's got piles of money," Danny said, returning with the book. "He's so rich he thinks we're all after his money. That's what my father says. That's why we never go visit them. Who wants to go somewhere if people think you're only out for their money?"

"Okay, Danny, that's enough. Give the mouth a rest." She showed Marcus the address in the book: George Renfrew, Renfrew Construction and Equipment Company, Factory Road, Latham, New York.

"Can I write it down?" Marcus said.

"If your memory's like mine, you better."

Then he had to ask for paper and pencil.

"Danny," Mrs. Belco said in some exasperation, "help this boy. And if you're thinking about the phone," she added to Marcus, "don't plan to call from here. It's long-distance. You can pay for it yourself from a pay booth. Or your mother can make the call on your phone at home."

"Oh, sure," Marcus said eagerly. "Of course." He thanked her several times and copied down the address. Danny leaned over his shoulder as he wrote.

"You write the way I do—chicken tracks," Danny said. "I'll see you in Bradford sometimes, okay? Listen, if you and your mother go visit Cousin George, invite me along. Maybe the two of us can get him to give us a ride on his big boat."

And Mrs. Belco had a last word of advice as he started for the door. "Tell your mother if she's thinking of getting anything going again with George, to forget it. Tell her he's in love with his business and has a wife and a couple of kids besides."

FIFTEEN

THE BUS TO LATHAM was dark and dirty, the windows unwashed, streaked with mud so that Marcus, gazing out, saw the countryside through a chalky haze. The trip took four hours, and the bus stopped so many times that Marcus, who had been trying to keep count and remember each town along the way, gave up in despair. The bus was never more than a quarter full and no one sat next to him at any time. He couldn't understand why the bus kept stopping and starting, and nobody got on, or only one or two people. If he'd had enough money he would have told the driver to go straight through to Latham . . . *That's right, driver, this is an emergency. My father will take care of the bill. He's the richest man in Latham* . . .

As the morning wore on and they got closer to Latham he thought of the letter he'd tried to write to his father. It had been impossible; he couldn't put his feelings into words. The harder he tried, the worse it got. So this morning, instead of going to school he had left Sally a brief note fastened to the refrigerator with a magnet. "Dear Mom, I went to see my father, but don't worry, I'll be home tonight. I love you. Marcus." Then he had gone downtown to the bus station, where his luck held and there was a bus leaving for Latham within the hour.

If only the bus would hurry! He tapped his feet, stared out the window, wriggled around uncomfortably on the hard plastic seat, and chewed stick after stick of gum. He'd never been so impatient in his life as he was now with this slow, creeping, dismal bus. He had waited for so long to meet his father, and now that he was so close, he felt he couldn't wait any longer. Impatience, a sense of excitement and impending joy overwhelmed him. He was so tantalizingly close to the most important moment of his life. But still the bus crept along at its snail's pace.

Renfrew Construction and Equipment Company was situated on the outskirts of the city, on Highway 27 leading to Whitestown. Marcus walked and then ran from where the bus let him off. The wind at his back thrust him along. He jogged till his ankles began to ache, walked, then jogged again. With each step he felt better and better. His ankles stopped aching, the twitch left his side, he felt he could run forever. He seemed to be flying, the ground passed effortlessly under his feet, and he stretched out his arms, rushing toward the meeting with his father. He ran past gas stations, warehouses, diners, furniture stores, car lots. He must have passed a hundred buildings before he came to Renfrew Construction and Equipment Company.

First, there was the sign on the road the size of a billboard, and then in front of a two-storied, glass-enclosed showroom and office were rows of huge yellow machinery. Earth-moving machines, cranes, scrapers, bulldozers, back hoes, rollers. And on the side of every piece of equipment his father's name— RENFREW CONSTRUCTION CO. It was his name, too!

He pushed open the glass door. A telephone was ringing. Voices came from the back of the building. He was in a large high-ceiling room, part office, part showroom, with several of the huge yellow machines, glistening, perfect, silent. The office was separated from the showroom by half a dozen large vinyl chairs and a dark vinyl couch.

A tall, skinny woman sat behind the desk, speaking into the phone. A name plate on the desk said NEILIE MORGAN. Bracelets flashed on her arms as she made notes on a pad. She nodded at Marcus and hung up the phone. "Okay, what can I do for you?"

"I want to see Mr. Renfrew."

She looked at him doubtfully. "The boss? What do you want?"

"I want to talk to him."

"Well, what about? He's a busy man. He's not here now."

"Will he be back pretty soon?"

Neilie Morgan shrugged. "He comes and goes."

"I'll wait," Marcus said.

"Suit yourself," she said, returning to the ringing phone.

He listened as she instructed first one caller, then another where they were to go next and what to do when they finished the jobs they were on. "Now, listen," she said sharply at one point, working her pencil into her hair, "you know you can't do that! George will have your neck." She listened. "My neck, too!"

She hung up, making a disgusted sound. The phone rang again.

In a lull between calls she asked Marcus again why he was there. "Business or personal?" she said, smiling a little. "You don't look like a businessman to me."

"It's personal," he said, glancing down at the *Iron Age* magazine on the table next to him.

"Well, what could this personal matter possibly be about?" she said.

Marcus shook his head. What he had to say, he would say only to his father.

Later when one of the salesmen brought Neilie Morgan afternoon coffee and a danish pastry she offered to share both with Marcus. He refused politely and immediately was beset with the most awful hunger pangs. He hadn't eaten since he'd left home that morning. There was a Coke machine in the corridor leading to the back of the building. "I'm going to get a Coke," he said. "If Mr. Renfrew—"

"I know," she said. "If Mr. Renfrew calls, there's an important person waiting to see him."

Marcus returned swiftly with the can of soda. "Has Mr. Renfrew been here while I was gone? Has he called?"

Neilie Morgan laughed, the bracelets and necklaces jingling. "You think he moves like a jet? You'll see him when he comes, don't worry. He'll hang around for a few moments. You sure you're not looking for a job, because I can tell you right now. We don't hire boys, not even good-looking boys like you."

"That's okay," he said, flushing. "I don't want a job." Sipping his soda as slowly as he could to make

176

it last, he wondered what Neilie Morgan would say when she discovered he was the boss's son.

Men in work clothes and dusty engineer's boots came and went in the office, all asking for George, but accepting orders from Neilie Morgan. "Who's the kid, Neilie?" one of the men said. "When George starts to hire them that young, I quit."

"Don't be surprised," she said. "The kind of work some of you guys do, a kid would be ashamed if he couldn't do better."

The man gave Marcus a wink. "If this kid wants my job, he can start right now."

It was impossible for Marcus to sit still. He jumped each time someone entered, and when the phone rang, he was on the edge of his seat. "Was that Mr. Renfrew?" he asked. Neilie Morgan finally told him she'd had enough.

"If you jump up one more time and ask me about Mr. Renfrew, I'm going to fly through the roof. Honest, I can't get my work done. Why don't you be a good kid and wait outside. I'll call you the moment Mr. Renfrew comes."

"You'll really call me the minute he comes in?"

"On my Boy Scout word of honor," she said.

Sitting outside, Marcus could hear the phone ringing and watch the men going in and out. How would he know if one of them was his father? What if Neilie Morgan forgot about him, and his father came and left? He would have run in and asked her ten times more, but he didn't want to irritate her again. He walked around the graveled lot, staring up at the big machines. His stomach growled and he looked longingly across the road at a hamburger stand, but he didn't dare leave, even for five minutes.

After what seemed like hours, Neilie Morgan came to the door. "You still here?" He was sitting on the concrete stairs, scuffing gravel. "Mr. Renfrew called. He's not coming back in today."

"What?" Marcus said, alarmed.

"Sorry. Come back tomorrow." She turned to go inside.

"Wait. Miss Morgan—" He had to see his father today. "Did you tell him I was here? Did you tell him I was waiting to see him? Does he want to meet me somewhere?"

"Sure he does," she said, a half smile on her lips. "I said there was a guy here from the Department of Transportation with a million-dollar contract." She opened the door. "Look, son, I told the boss there was a kid here waiting for him and I didn't know your business because you didn't tell me. He said to give you a dollar for the Boy Scouts or whatever you're collecting for."

Marcus shook his head. "No, I've got to see him today. I mean it. I can't come back tomorrow."

"Well," she said, lifting her shoulders. "I'm sorry." She closed the door and went back into her office. Through the glass window he could see her talking on the phone again.

He wandered around the side of the building to the sheds in back where mechanics were working on the machines. He stopped to watch a man welding the broken metal teeth of a big shovel. The man lifted his helmet. "Are you looking at the arc?" he yelled. "Get out of here, or you're going to go blind young." He dropped his helmet again.

Depressed, Marcus looked out across the open sheds where pipe and iron and heavy timbers were stacked. He didn't know what to do now. Maybe he could sleep in one of these sheds that night, or maybe he ought to return to the bus station and sleep there on a bench. In either case he had to call Sally and tell her he was staying in Latham another day. She wouldn't like that very much. "What about school?" she'd say. "You've already missed so much."

The man had stopped welding and had removed his helmet and gloves and was rubbing his eyes. "You still hanging around here, kid?"

"I wanted to see Mr. Renfrew."

"The boss—what do you want to find him for?"

"I just want to talk to him."

"He won't hire you."

Why did they all think he wanted a job? "It's not that." He turned away, too discouraged to explain.

"Hey, kid." The welder called him back. "You really want to find Renfrew?" Marcus nodded. "Well, when he isn't here he's at his house out on Riverview Terrace, where all the doctors and bankers have their big houses. Renfrew started out like the rest of us, but he's right up there now."

Following the welder's instructions, Marcus walked back along the highway for what seemed like miles, at last turning toward the river, which was broad and flat, the color of steel under the low, cloudy sky. He was hungry and hot, but he couldn't stop to eat or drink or rest. He'd been trying for so long that he

179

began to feel that he would go on and on, chasing his father, just missing him, never finding him, always being told to go somewhere else. As he got closer to the river, the sounds of the highway were muffled. There wasn't a soul in sight. Only expensive sprawling houses, widely spaced like jewels on immense green velvet lawns.

The Renfrew mailbox, like all the others along Riverview Terrace, hung from a heavy wood and chain scaffold, black and as big as a doghouse. A long driveway curved toward closed double garage doors. The house was still. Marcus rang the bell and heard chimes echoing inside. When no one came to the door he sat on the ground next to the swaying mailbox, his knees up under his chin. He thought of the huge letters these people must get. Fat letters for rich people. Or maybe their dogs slept in there, guarding the property and the money. Everything around Marcus seemed excessive and unreal. Everything bulged. The house with its extra-thick split cedar siding, and the immense protruding bay window; even the mortar oozed out from between the white bricks of the chimney. His father must be really rich. Marcus thought he'd probably have to learn how to be rich, too.

He waited for a long time, as he'd been waiting all day, and still nobody came. The ground beneath him grew chill and the sun dropped. Except for an occasional passing car, he was completely alone.

The first person to appear was a girl of about nine who got off a small blue bus with the words RED

CREEK SCHOOL on the side. She wore a dark blue parka with a fur collar. "You're sitting on my property," she said. Marcus told her he was waiting for George Renfrew. "That's my father. What's your name?"

"Marcus," he said.

She stood there, watching him. "Why are you sitting on the ground?"

"It's more comfortable than standing." It occurred to him that this girl was his half sister. He looked at her closely to see if they resembled each other.

"My mother's going to be home soon," she said. "And my brother Steven. Do you know my brother Steven?"

Marcus shook his head. So there was a boy as well.

The girl went into the house, and he was alone again.

In a little while a woman appeared in a small yellow sports car, pulling swiftly into the driveway. She barely glanced at Marcus. The garage doors opened and closed automatically, and she, too, disappeared into the house.

He thought that he would sit there for however long he had to. If his father didn't show up, or if nobody came out to talk to him, he'd sit there all night. He'd sit and wait till the next morning, or the morning after. He'd sit there till he grew roots, but he was going to see his father.

Across the road, a girl who appeared to be about his own age had come around the end of a brick house. She was carrying a tennis racket and seemed to be staring at him suspiciously. He didn't move, but looked back at her through narrowed eyes. When she found out who he really was, she'd probably fall all over herself to be nice to him.

Soon a brown and gold stationwagon slowed and turned into the driveway. A man and a boy were in the front seat. As the wagon passed him, Marcus discovered that he couldn't move his neck, or turn his head. He stared fixedly ahead of him. He thought the man had glanced at him, but he couldn't be sure.

When Marcus finally turned around, the stationwagon was parked in the driveway. The man and the boy got out and walked into the house through a side door. They were all inside now, the man and the woman and the two children. Marcus had never anticipated things happening this way. What if no one came out to talk to him? Should he go up to the house, ring the bell again, ask for Mr. Renfrew, or should he wait there a while longer.

He stood up, looking toward the wide, curtained bay window. The thought of leaving, of going home, passed through his mind. His stomach tightened. He'd come there to see his father. He couldn't even be sure that was the man who'd driven the wagon.

The front door slammed. The boy came outside. He was blond and skinny. He walked slowly toward Marcus. "What do you want?" he demanded when he was a few feet away. He wore a thick leather band on his left wrist.

Marcus glanced over the boy's shoulder, as if he barely recognized his existence. "George Renfrew," he said. "Is he inside there? Tell him I'm here."

"Who's here?" the boy said. "Who are you?"

"I want to see George Renfrew," Marcus said, his voice rising.

"You better get off our property," the boy said.

Marcus didn't answer. He sat down again near the mailbox and stared across the road.

"You must be some kind of freak," the boy said. He threw a piece of gravel into the road, then he left. The door slammed. Everything was quiet again. Marcus imagined them all inside, eating, while he sat here, famished and cold. The conviction grew on him that his father was inside, that the man who had driven the stationwagon was George Renfrew.

A dog began barking behind him. Marcus turned. A big brown and white collie was bounding down the driveway, barking at Marcus. Behind the dog was the man he had glimpsed in the stationwagon. Marcus felt his eyes beginning to unfocus as he tried to appear calm.

"You looking for me?" The man was very tall, with a broad high forehead and tight curly hair. He wore a golfer's green trousers and a yellow sports shirt with a little red alligator over the pocket. He had a drink in his hand.

Marcus scrambled up, the dog barking at his feet.

"Down, Rusty." The man grabbed the dog by the ears. "Stop that, I say! What can I do for you?" he said to Marcus. "My boy tells me you want to speak to me." He waved to someone in a passing car. "Are you the new newsboy? Why didn't you come up to the house?" He opened the huge metal mailbox and drew out a newspaper. "Do I owe you for this?"

The dog lay at the man's feet, watching Marcus.

"Are you George Renfrew?" Marcus said, in a barely audible voice.

"Right. Who are you?"

"I'm—Marcus." His eyes, which had been wandering, finally focused on his father's face. He'd imagined this meeting so many times. Dreaming, it had always been simple enough to say those words: *I'm Marcus.* And then he'd imagined the look of recognition that would slowly spread across his father's face, followed by an explosion of feeling and joy. And his father embracing his son . . . *Marcus, my son, my son . . .*

"Well?" Renfrew said, "what's the pitch?"

"I'm Marcus Rosenbloom," Marcus said urgently.

"Yes?" The man's face showed neither recognition nor pleasure. "How much do I owe you, Rosenbloom?" A little smile flickered at the corners of his mouth.

"I'm not the newsboy. I'm Marcus Rosenbloom," he said again.

Renfrew opened the folded newspaper. "Should I know you? What's your business here?"

Marcus had the awful feeling that he'd somehow come to the wrong city, the wrong house, the wrong man. He glanced at the mailbox, at the name REN-FREW in large gold letters. "Ahh—ahh—are you M-Mr. Renfrew?" He couldn't control the shaking of his voice, his whole body was vibrating like a missing engine, coughing and stammering. "Are you r-really Mr. Renfrew? *George* Renfrew?"

The man stepped toward him and gripped Marcus's shoulder. "What's the matter with you, boy? Speak up. Who are you? I don't have all day for kid games."

Then he seemed to make a connection. "Are you the kid who was hanging around in our office today?"

"My mother's name is Sally Rosenbloom," Marcus said. He was sure now that he had made a terrible mistake. He had somehow come to the wrong place. This was a George Renfrew, but not the right one. Not his father. This man couldn't be his father.

But now Renfrew was looking at him in a new way. "Sally Rosenbloom," he said. "Sally Rosenbloom!" Marcus winced. His mother's name on Renfrew's lips seemed foreign, strange, painfully exciting. "Where the hell is Sally? Is she here?" He looked around as if expecting to see Sally step out from behind the hedge.

"She's home," Marcus said.

"She sent you here," Renfrew said. "I'll be damned. What's this all about? I haven't seen Sally in a dog's years. Why'd she send you?"

Marcus shook his head violently. "No! It was my idea to come here. Sally didn't want me to come, but I came anyway!"

Renfrew looked at him closely. "She didn't want you to come, but you came anyway," he repeated slowly. "Why?"

"She couldn't keep me from seeing my own father." As he said the words Marcus's shoulders began to shake uncontrollably. He turned his face away, ashamed of crying in front of his father. He had never thought this would happen. "I never cry anymore," he wept. It was just this moment—this wonderful moment. He wiped his cheeks—his father's face blurred by the tears.

"You're Sally's son?" his father said.

185

"Your son," Marcus said hoarsely.

His father made a disclaiming gesture, then looking around, he said quietly, "Wait here. I'll get the car and we'll take a ride and talk."

SIXTEEN

MARCUS SAT in the front of the stationwagon next to his father. In the back were a brassbound wooden box, rolled-up blueprints, several yellow construction hats, a pair of lace-up engineer's boots, and a set of golf clubs. "Let's ride around for a while," his father said. "We'll talk." Then he was silent for a long time.

Marcus looked out at the passing countryside. There were things he wanted to say to his father, questions to ask. He wanted to tell his father about school, his drug arrest, about dieting, and all the dreams of meeting him. He wanted to know if his father had ever thought about *him*, and what he felt now that they were together.

His father drove fast and easily, one hand on the steering wheel. "This is a really comfortable stationwagon," Marcus said, breaking the silence. He stretched out his legs and leaned back, emulating his father's easy posture. "My Uncle Al has a VW bug, but there's no room in that. This is a real car."

"It's a good enough car," his father said briefly. "Let's get this straight now. How old did you say you were?"

"Nearly fourteen," Marcus said, pulling himself up straight. "Some people think I look older than my age." He laughed. "Some people even think I act older than my age," he added ebulliently. He felt high on happiness. He expanded in the nearness of his father, in this great moment he'd dreamed of and waited for so long. He told his father how independent he was. "Sally doesn't tell me anything. I came here by myself. I go anywhere I want. Sally doesn't say anything, as long as I act responsible. I've been taking care of myself ever since I was a little kid."

"You call your mother Sally?"

Marcus nodded. "I've called her Sally all my life."

"That sounds like one of her goofy ideas all right. So what's Sally told you about me?"

"Nothing," Marcus said. "My mother never talked about you."

"Just enough to send you running here, huh?"

Marcus reached over to the dashboard and fiddled with the knobs and dials on the radio. "I've been thinking about meeting you for a long time," he said. "Sally never wanted me to come. It was all my own idea. I had to really fight with her to make her even tell me your name." He clenched his fists. "It wasn't easy. I didn't even know your name till a few weeks ago."

His father rubbed a hand along his jaw. His face was deeply tanned, with white lines etched across his forehead and around his eyes. "What year were you born?" And then he wanted to know if Sally was married, and were there any other children.

He pulled the car over to the shoulder of the road,

and took a pack of cigarettes out of the side pocket of his jacket. "You smoke?" Marcus shook his head. "It's a rotten habit," his father said, "but I've got it. I told Steve if he didn't smoke till he was twenty-one I'd give him a thousand bucks. Same thing with booze. When he's twenty-one he picks up another thousand if he's stayed clean till then. I figure by then he might fool with it a little, but he'll never get the habit as bad as me. I started smoking when I was fourteen—"

"My age," Marcus interrupted eagerly.

His father looked over at him. "Yeah," he said. "So you say Sally didn't want you to come here?"

"That's right." Marcus tried to meet his father's eyes, but Renfrew was staring out the window, puffing on his cigarette. "She said I'd only be hurt, that seeing you wouldn't be good—" His voice dropped. Maybe he'd hurt his father's feelings saying that. He stared anxiously at the man. "I never thought that way."

Renfrew started the car again. "Your mother sure knows how to surprise a man."

"It wasn't her idea."

"All these years—I practically forgot all about Sally Rosenbloom, for Christ sake, and now suddenly *you* pop up with this story." He looked deeply at Marcus. "You my son?" He sighed and shook his head. "Well, okay, let's forget it for now. What do you say we get something to eat? You hungry?"

Marcus said, "I haven't eaten all day." But the odd thing was that his hunger pangs had disappeared. He actually felt as full as if he'd just eaten a meal.

As they drove his father pointed to a school, a

parking lot, a shopping center, and several small buildings. "I built that center. I built all that. I run the biggest general construction company in this part of the state. Everybody knows George Renfrew. It's my own business, I built it with my own hands, started small and worked like a dog for everything I've got."

"I know," Marcus said. "You've got a lot of trucks and machines, I saw them. I like everything that belongs to you." He watched his father's hands as he drove, imagining himself as part of his father's life. Going everywhere with him in this stationwagon . . . *What do you think, Marcus, should we take on this job?* . . . He was aware in another part of his mind that his father hadn't said much to him yet about how he really felt about Marcus's appearing. But Marcus understood. He'd caught his father by surprise. His father was getting used to him. They had plenty of time for everything.

His father parked outside a silver-sided diner. "This is the only place to eat in town," he said. As they got out of the car he stopped to greet a balding man unlocking a Cadillac. "How you doing, Jim?" his father said. "Been to Las Vegas lately?" The two men laughed heartily at some private joke.

Marcus stood next to his father, wanting to pinch himself as he realized over and over that he was there, with his father.

"How do you like that car?" his father said as the man drove away.

"Nice," Marcus said.

"That man is a state senator," his father said. "He's going to be a judge someday."

"Is he a friend of yours?" Marcus said respectfully.

"We've done business," his father said. He led the way toward the diner, greeting the cashier, the waitress, the people sitting at the counter. His father knew everyone. When they were seated in a booth, his father ordered hamburgers, a double order of french fries, coffee for himself and a vanilla malted for Marcus. Marcus hated vanilla, but he didn't say anything. He thought it was wonderful that his father had ordered for him. It gave him a glow, made him feel warm and talkative.

"I've been watching my weight," he said. "I've had this little weight problem for quite a while. I put on fat right here—" He patted his middle. "So I've been cutting down on stuff. First I tried to go without lunch, but that didn't work so good. Now I just eat less all around. Maybe I won't have that vanilla malted. And I won't eat many french fries. I've been trying to cut right down on ice cream and fried stuff. The only good thing about my weight is that I'm tall. I'm nearly as tall as you. Sally only comes up to here on me." He pointed to his chin. "I'm the tallest kid in my class. A lot of people, especially this one girl who's the sister of my best friend, guessed that my father must be really tall, because I'm such a tall kid."

"You like to talk, don't you?" his father said.

Marcus half laughed. He felt embarrassed that he'd been blabbing that way. "Me? I don't talk all the time. Not that much, it's just that I have so much to tell you."

"As I remember it, your mother was a big talker, too. She used to talk my ears off about everything. I never knew a girl who could get so excited about so many things that didn't concern her. The starving masses in India! The poor slobs in this country, and the poor slobs in that country."

Marcus reached for a second hamburger. He felt that he ought to defend Sally, but at the same time he wanted to be agreeable and friendly, not argumentative.

"I like a boy who eats," his father said, holding up his hand to the waitress for two more hamburgers. "It's a sign of good health. I can't stand these people who are always dieting. Cottage cheese and carrots!"

"Maybe I will have that vanilla drink," Marcus said. If his father liked a good appetite, then he'd show what a good appetite really was. He unwrapped the straw, crumpled the paper. His father finished his coffee while Marcus was still drinking the malted. It was too sweet for him, but he sipped it up fast, trying not to taste the flavoring.

"You came here by bus, is that right?" his father said.

Marcus nodded. "It took four hours." He looked up at the fly-specked clock over the counter. "I guess Sally will be home from work by now. I left her a note I was coming because I just made up my mind in a hurry. But she won't be mad. I can go where I want to go. If I wanted to come live here, I could.

Sally would say, 'Marcus, it's up to you. Make your own decision.' That's the way she's always been."

His father paused in the act of shaking another cigarette out of his pack. "Now hold on a minute. Is that what this visit is all about? Am I starting to get the picture really clear now? Sally wants you to come here and live with me. That's what's behind this sudden visit? And what other plans does Miss Rosenbloom have?" He was smiling and Marcus found it impossible to resist that wide friendly smile.

"She'd like to travel," he said. "If she didn't have to think about me and school, she'd go with Bill when he travels."

"Bill," his father said. "Who's he?"

"Sally's friend. My friend, too. He plays the trumpet and travels all over the world. He's a real nice guy."

"So Bill's the boyfriend and your mother would like to see you off her hands. Am I getting the picture?"

"Hey, no," Marcus said. He had a moment of confusion, a feeling of having been disloyal to Sally. He wanted to make things clear. "Sally is good, she's a good mother. She's the best, we get along okay. I'm not complaining. I was just trying to explain about stuff—" He gestured, trying to encompass the idea of him and his father. "About you and me."

"You and me," his father repeated, making the words sound awkward and impossible. He sensed his father's attention drifting away from him. He felt the whole marvelous day somehow escaping him. The sense of joy, the high of knowing he'd finally found his father, was drifting away like smoke. He wanted to wrench his father's attention back to him, to capture again that intense joy and expectation. He thought of Sally and what she would say when he came home, and then he remembered her face and her eyes after the hearing before Dr. Holley. "What you did was so good," she had said. "I was so proud of my son, Marcus."

Yes, she'd been proud; he wanted his father to look at him like that. "I was arrested," he said. His father's eyes focused on him.

"Arrested! What the hell for?"

He had his father's attention again. He told him the whole story. He told him how Dorrity and Phillips had lied, and how he himself, although it put him in bad trouble, refused to tattle on them, refused to get them into trouble. All the time he was talking he felt stronger, surer, and searched his father's face for signs of approval. His father would see now that he had a son worthy of being his son, worthy of being acknowledged, worthy of being a Renfrew . . . *Marcus, I'm proud of you. You set a fine example . . .*

His father stared at him, then shook his head slowly from side to side. "I don't believe it. You kids today—"

"It's all true," Marcus said eagerly. "Sally never thought they would lie like that, either."

"I don't believe a kid can be as big as you and be so dumb. What the hell did you think they were going to do? You think those two other kids are going around saying, 'Isn't Marcus wonderful? He didn't give us away!' The hell they are. They're laughing up their sleeves because they're home free, and you got stuck with the bag. Didn't anybody ever tell you that in this world you watch out for number one? You understand what I'm saying?"

It was a painful moment. "I never thought of it like that," Marcus said.

Renfrew drained his coffee cup. "I don't see how your mother let you get away with that. If you were my kid, I sure as hell—" He broke off, gave a wry grin, and snapped his fingers at the waitress for another cup of coffee.

An older man with a wide red face and thinning white hair stopped to talk to his father. They talked about roads, property values, and rights of way. Half listening, Marcus began to imagine how he and his father appeared to this man. Did the man realize they were father and son? He had only to look at Renfrew and then at Marcus to draw the inevitable conclusion. Father and son . . . both tall . . . same curly hair . . . yes, alike as two peas in a pod. Sitting in a diner, sharing a cup of coffee, both of them dusty, tired, but feeling good after a hard, satisfying day's work . . . *I like a man who can work hard and eat hard*, his father often said, *it's a sign of health*. Work hard, eat hard, play hard, that was the Renfrew credo. He and his father often stopped here after work for a bite on the way home. He was going to school half days of course, but working with his father the rest of the time, really learning all about the construction business. When they stopped they talked about the work, and his father explained things that were important for him to learn . . . *In this world,* his father said, *you have to be rough, none of this bleeding heart stuff* . . .

The older man was speaking to him. "What's that?" Marcus said politely.

"I said, How do you like Latham, young fellow? Your uncle tells me you're here for the day for a visit."

Marcus stared at the broad red face. He didn't know what to say. His uncle? His father caught his eye, giving him a warning glance. "Yes, sir," Marcus got out. "I like it a lot."

"You keep your eyes on your Uncle George here," the older man said, clapping Renfrew on the shoulder, "and if you're lucky you'll pick up a little know-how and you might someday get to be about half as successful a man as he is. Got to run fast, though." He winked at Marcus. "Right, George? Well, I'll be seeing you."

When he left, Marcus stirred the straw round and round in his empty glass. "Why did you tell him I was your nephew?"

His father pushed the coffee cup away impatiently. "Look, let's get things straight. I've fed you, I've driven you around town, I've listened to your stories. I've got nothing against you, Marcus, but let me ask you something flat out—what makes you so damn sure you really are my kid?"

Marcus felt a thud deep inside him, as if a steel ball had swept against his ribs. "Sally told me," he said at last.

"Did it ever occur to you that she could be wrong?"

"No," Marcus said. "No."

His father smiled, that broad white smile. "Come on, you're a smart kid. Maybe there is a connection, but look at things from my viewpoint. I've got a family. I'm a well-known businessman. Around here, people know me, they know my family, they look up to me. Do I have to spell it out for you? I've got to think about my family first. What would they think if I suddenly popped up with you—this is Marcus Rosenbloom, everybody, he says he's my son by another woman. What effect do you think that's going to have on them?"

Marcus took a limp french fry and dipped it in ketchup and ate it. He ate another one and another one. There was something hard and immovable lodged under his breastbone. He wasn't hungry, but he keep eating limp french fries dipped in ketchup.

"Just remember I didn't even know about you till this afternoon. I'm not used to this—this idea of maybe having another son. I don't know if I'll ever get used to it."

"Okay," Marcus said. He began to feel a little sick from the french fries. He got up and walked to the door. His arms and legs were stiff and the back of his head felt curiously numb. Outside, in the parking lot it was dark. Street lights were on. His father came out of the diner and the door pinged shut. He smiled warmly at Marcus. "Come on, get in the car." And then when they were seated, "Where to, now?"

"I guess I better go back to the bus terminal," Marcus said. "I should go home." Stupidly he kept hoping that his father would say or do something to make everything right, to bring back the early bright promise of the day.

"The bus station. Right," his father said cheerfully. "Your mother's probably getting worried about you." The car jounced over the gravel and then moved smoothly into the main road. "You gave me a real jolt this afternoon, showing up out of nowhere," his father said. "I didn't even know you existed. I'll be truthful with you—that time about when you were born, I was sure Sally had done something about it, about her pregnancy, I mean. I told her a long time before, right in the beginning, go see a doctor, get it taken care of. I told her I'd take care of everything, money and all that. I told her I didn't want a kid, I wasn't ready for anything like that. I didn't have much, then, but I gave her money. Wouldn't you know, she sent it back. It came to my folks' store. I thought, that's Sally for you. Always had to do things her own way. But I never for a moment thought she went through with it and had the kid. But here you are, aren't you?"

Marcus rolled down his window. For a moment he thought he was going to throw up, ketchup, french fries, vanilla malted, greasy hamburgers, all of it. He clutched his stomach, and gulped in fresh air.

"Maybe I'm talking a little over your head, Marcus, but that's the way things are, you can't always be a nice guy. In my line of work I've had to be rough lots of times, fire guys, tell people to get out of my way. Sally did what she wanted to. That's all right, but it's her business, not mine." All the way to the bus station, his father talked and Marcus was silent. "I'm a fair man, I want to do what's fair. If Sally needs money, if she gets in a jam, tell her to get in touch with me at the office. The same goes for you. Listen, later on if you go to college, come see me, I can help you out."

At the bus station he pulled into a parking place and half turned toward Marcus. "So," he said. "I guess we understand each other now." He put a hand on Marcus's shoulder and smiled at him. "What do you say now? Plain talk throw you?"

Marcus shrugged off his hand awkwardly. "I've got to find out about my bus."

Renfrew followed him into the station and insisted on buying Marcus's ticket home. There was a half-hour wait. "Want a candy bar?" his father said.

"No," Marcus said. He didn't think he'd ever be hungry again. His stomach felt awful. The thought of the meal he'd eaten in the diner sent waves of queasiness sloshing over him.

They walked up and down the big echoing station. Rows of empty plastic chairs in the middle of the room. A gift shop behind big plate-glass windows. "I don't want you to go away feeling bad," his father said.

Marcus noted the time in London on the international clock on the far wall. London, Latham, he thought vaguely. He was trying not to think, not to feel.

His father pulled a roll of green bills out of his pocket and extracted a twenty. "Here, get yourself something, anything you want."

A flash of clean anger cleared away Marcus's vagueness. He pushed away the proferred money. "No. I don't want it."

Renfrew tried to shove the bill into his hand. "Don't be stubborn, Marcus. Anybody offers you money, grab it. Go on, you can always use money. You're not that much above us all." He stuffed the bill into Marcus's shirt pocket. "I'd like to get you something, also," he said.

"I don't want any candy," Marcus said. "I don't want anything."

"Not candy, something real," his father said. "I noticed you don't have a watch."

Marcus felt the weight of the twenty-dollar bill in his pocket. "I don't need one, I've got a good sense of time."

"Every boy should have a wristwatch. I got my first one when I was thirteen for helping my father after school in his store. Steven got his when he was ten." As he spoke, he steered Marcus into the gift shop and toward a revolving tray of watches laid out on purple velvet beds. "Pick one out," his father said. "Don't be bashful. Which one do you like?"

Marcus shook his head. He was growing hotter and hotter. "I said I don't want anything."

"I want you to have a watch," his father insisted. "We'll take this one," he said to the woman behind the counter. He pointed to one with a round gold face, with roman numerals and a small square window for the date. It had luminous hands and a leather strap.

"That's our most popular one," the woman said. "Fifteen jewels. Shockproof and water-resistant, and it never needs winding, you know. It runs on a battery."

"Tell it to this boy, he's a real screwball. Here I'm ready to buy him the best watch in the place, and he doesn't want it. He acts like I'm trying to poison him. Some people don't know when they're well off."

She smiled politely and took the two twenty-dollar bills he handed her, giving him back a few coins. She took the watch off its velvet bed and held it out to Marcus. "It's an awfully nice watch," she said in a kind way. "I hope you enjoy wearing it."

Marcus smiled painfully and accepted the watch.

"You're a stubborn kid, you know that," his father said as Marcus held the watch, but didn't put it on.

"I guess so," Marcus said. Stubborn kid? Maybe. He was probably a lot more stubborn than he knew. He saw himself in the glass door as they walked toward it. He hardly recognized himself. Was that tall, big-boned boy with red cheeks and wild hair Marcus? Stubborn Marcus. He thought of all the ideas he'd had about himself. He'd put himself down to the bottom of the heap as a fat slob and lifted himself to the top of the skies as a tall, dashing cavalier. Marcus the Insignificant, and Marcus the Magnificent. Up and down, high and low he'd gone, grasping for the real Marcus who always seemed out of reach. A stubborn kid? A jerk? Strong and beautiful? Who was he?

He thought how much he'd wanted his father, how

his whole life, his balance, his very self, had seemed to depend on finding his father and being with him. Now he was leaving his father, and it didn't seem to matter at all. We're strangers, he thought—my father and I. We don't know each other, we don't understand each other, we don't even think the same things are important.

Later, as the bus left Latham behind, he looked out the window and in the light of neon signs on gas stations and motels saw again how flat the country was, flat and uninteresting. He remembered how Latham had looked that morning—filled with the shine and glitter of something indescribably wonderful—the dream of his father.

The bus made him drowsy and he caught himself dreaming of the way the meeting with his father might have gone.

In his dreams and fantasies he'd created his father as anything he wanted him to be—a mixture of Superman, 007, and Father of the Year. But he couldn't do that anymore. He made himself stop pretending. His father was too real in his mind now, for that kind of thing. Marcus didn't think he really liked his father at all. Maybe—and this was an odd and startling thought—maybe his father just wasn't his kind of person. His or Sally's.

His father was hard-driving and interested in being rich. Bill wasn't like that. He was kinder and interested in other people, interested in his music. His mother was kind, too, but she liked to do things her own way. She was strong-minded.

He thought of all the people he cared about. Bernie was dogged and practical. Vivian was enthusiastic, a caring sort of person. Wendy was intense, a little weird, but she had feelings. His Grandma May was brisk, loving, and lots of fun.

For a moment he was able to see them all clearly, but if he let himself think about any one too long, things blurred and changed. People were like clouds in the sky, always shifting, never remaining exactly the same.

And what about himself? All those ideas, all those fantasies and self-deceptive glimpses of himself in bus windows and mirrors and store fronts. All the things he'd made himself in his dreams. What kind of person was he really?

He was a searcher and a doer. He liked the idea. He had searched for his father and found him. That was good. And he was a person who had principles and stuck up for them, no matter what. He'd been scared at the hearing, but he'd stuck to his ideas, his principles; nobody had made him say something he thought was wrong.

Maybe, too, he was a person who found out things for himself and was able to face the truth and go on. The truth was, his father didn't care about him. He was an embarrassment to his father. His father had tried to buy him off with a twenty-dollar bill and a forty-dollar watch.

Marcus took the twenty-dollar bill from his pocket and laid it on his lap next to the watch and looked at them both for a long time. The twenty-dollar man, he thought, remembering the ease with which his father had peeled off twenty-dollar bills from the fat roll he carried.

When the bus pulled into his home depot, Marcus got off, leaving the watch and the twenty-dollar bill behind him on the seat.

635329